THE
SUCCESSOR

Ismail Kadare was born in 1936 in Gjirokaster, in the south of Albania. He studied in Tirana and Moscow, returning to Albania in 1960 after the country broke ties with the Soviet Union. He became a journalist and published poet, and his first novel, *The General of the Dead Army*, immediately established him as a brilliant writer. Translations of his novels have since been published in more than forty countries, and in 2005 he became the first winner of the Man Booker International Prize.

David Bellos, a Professor of French and Comparative Literature, is a writer and translator who has translated five of Kadare's novels and was winner of the 2005 Man Booker International Prize for Translation. He is currently working on Kadare's *Agamemnon's Daughter*, also to be published by Canongate.

Also by Ismail Kadare

THE
SUCCESSOR

ISMAIL KADARE

Translated from the French of
Tedi Papavrami by David Bellos

CANONGATE
Edinburgh · New York · Melbourne

First published in Great Britain in 2006 by
Canongate Books Ltd, 14 High Street,
Edinburgh EH1 1TE

First published in English in the United States in 2005 by
Arcade Publishing, Inc., New York
First published in Albanian as *Pasardhësi* by Shtëpia Botuese "55"
Published in France by Éditions Fayard as *Le Successeur*,
translated from the Albanian by Tedi Papavrami

This edition first published by Canongate Books Ltd in 2007

1

British Library Cataloguing-in-Publication Data
A catalogue record for this book is available on
request from the British Library

978 1 84195 887 3 (13-digit ISBN)
1 84195 887 5 (10-digit ISBN)

Designed by API

Printed and bound in Great Britain by
Clays Ltd, St Ives plc

www.canongate.co.uk

The events of this novel draw on the infinite well of human memory, whose treasures may be brought to the surface in any period, including our own. In view of this, any resemblance between the characters and circumstances of this tale and real people and events is inevitable.

Ismail Kadare

CONTENTS

THE
SUCCESSOR

ONE

A DEATH IN DECEMBER

1

The Designated Successor was found dead in his bedroom at dawn on December 14. Albanian television
made a brief announcement of the facts at noon:
"During the night of December 13, the Successor suc-
cumbed to a nervous depression and took his own life
with a firearm."

International news agencies circulated the
Albanian government's version of the story around
the world. Only later that afternoon, when Yugoslav
radio voiced a suspicion that the suicide might actually have been murder, did the wire services amend
their bulletins to allow for both versions of the event.

In the middle of the sky, which stretched as far as
the eye could see and carried the news far and wide,

stood a high clump of clouds like a celestial wrath.

Whereas the death shook the whole country, the absence of national mourning, and especially the unaltered television and radio schedules, failed to provoke the intended shock. Once their initial puzzlement had passed, people were persuaded by the explanation that was doing the rounds: despite the country's rejection of the cross, suicide remained implicitly just as blameworthy as it was in the Christian faith. What was more — and this was the main thing — throughout the autumn and especially after the onset of winter, people had begun to expect the Successor to topple.

2

Albanians had long been unaccustomed to the tolling of bells, so they looked next day for signs of mourning wherever they might be found — on the façades of government buildings, in the musical offerings broadcast by national radio, or on the face of their neighbour stuck in the long line outside the dairy. The nonappearance of flags at half-mast and the absence of funeral marches on the airwaves eventually peeled the scales from the eyes of those who had chosen to believe that things were just a bit behind schedule.

News agencies around the world persisted in reporting the event and in giving the two alternative explanations: suicide and murder.

In fact, it looked more and more as if the Successor had intentionally chosen to depart this sorry world in a particular way, wrapped in not one but two shrouds of mourning, as if he had decided to have himself hauled away by two black oxen, one being insufficient to his needs.

As they anxiously opened their morning papers, hoping to learn something more about the event, people were actually trying to fathom which of the two alternatives — self-inflicted death, or death inflicted by the hand of another — would affect them less harshly.

For lack of news in the media, people fell back on what was being repeated in after-dinner gossip all over town. The night of the Successor's death had been truly terrifying — and it was certainly not a figment of their imagination, for everyone had seen it. Lightning, downpours, and wild gusts of wind! It was no secret that after an autumn full of fears, the Successor had been going through a psychologically difficult time. The next day, in fact, he had been due to attend a decisive meeting of the Politburo where the errors he had to confess in his self-criticism would presumably have been forgiven.

But like so many people born under a cloud and who, on the very brink of salvation, slip and fall into the abyss, the Successor had been in too much of a hurry. He had penned a letter of apology for taking his leave and then ended his own life.

That night, the whole family had been at home. After supper, as he was on his way to bed, the Successor asked his wife to please wake him at eight in the morning. For her part, she who had found it impossible to sleep for weeks on end, as she would later admit, fell into a deep slumber that lasted all night. Her daughter, who had spotted light coming from under her father's bedroom door as late as two in the morning, when it went out, turned in to bed shortly thereafter. Nobody heard any noise whatsoever.

And that was pretty much all the information that emanated, or seemed to emanate, from the house of the deceased. But other stories seeped out from the gated compound — the *Bllok* — where state officials lived. If the night had indeed been particularly wet and windy, an unusual number of cars had nonetheless been seen entering and leaving the *Bllok*. The strangest thing was that around midnight, or maybe a little later, the silhouette of a man had been seen slipping into the residence of the deceased. A prominent member of the government . . . but it was forbidden to say . . . not under any circumstances . . . so, an extremely high-ranking official . . . had gone in . . . and come out again shortly thereafter . . .

3

The files on Albania lay mouldering under a thick coat of dust. That wasn't by any means the first time that such lack of rigour had been observed inside various intelligence agencies. As can be imagined, the observation carried more than a hint of criticism on the part of the ranking officers and spread a sense of guilt among the subordinates, who set about reopening said files, promising never to shirk their duties again.

What was known about Albania was mostly obsolete, and some of it was distinctly romanticised. A small nation whose name meant "Land of Eagles". An ancient people of the Balkan Peninsula, who had succeeded the Illyrians and perpetuated their tongue.

A new state that had emerged from the ruins of the Ottoman Empire at the dawn of the twentieth century. A land of three faiths: Catholic, Orthodox and Muslim, declared a monarchy under a minor German prince of the Protestant persuasion. Then a republic under the leadership of an Albanian bishop. Who was overthrown in a civil war led by the next king, this one a native. Who was overthrown in his turn by another sovereign — an Italian monarch, as it happened, who confiscated the Albanian crown and proclaimed himself "King of Italy and Albania and Emperor of Abyssinia". And finally, after that grotesque coupling, where for the first time in their history Albanians were led to constitute a state on an equal footing with Africans, came the outbreak of Communist dictatorship. With new friendships and bizarre alliances solemnly made and haughtily repudiated.

On that part of the story, in fact, and in particular on the two major squabbles, first with the Russians then with the Chinese, most of the files bore traces of subsequent revision. Several extra sheets had been slipped in, containing analyses, reflections, facts and forecasts, most of which ended in a question mark.

The addenda were mostly attempts to work out which way Albania would turn next: towards the West, or once again to the East? The answer was rendered even more uncertain by its being dependent on other questions for which answers had never been found. Was it in the West's interest to draw Albania into its bosom? Some position papers seemed to refer to the possibility of a secret accord between the Communist bloc and the West: We'll drop Albania — on condition you keep your hands off it too. One of the files even quoted a brief in which the issue was stated explicitly: Should the West risk alarming the Soviet camp by seducing poor little Albania, or keep the sweet talk for a better-endowed bride, namely Czechoslovakia?

But interest had manifestly waned as the years went by, and you could measure the growing distance by the resurgence of archaic and romantic terms in the notes and briefs in the agency files — words related to the royal fowl, the eagle, and to the age-old law book called the Canon of Lek, or *Kanun*.

All that seemed to be but a dress rehearsal for what would take place years later, when Albania broke off relations with China. The same questions would be asked, the same answers suggested, and apart from the fact that it was all a bit more bland, and that the word "Poland" replaced "Czechoslovakia", the conclusions were roughly the same as before.

The death of the Successor that cold December was therefore the third time the files on Albania had been dusted off. Supervisors in various intelligence agencies grew ever more critical of their clerks: we've had enough folklore, and to hell with your birds of prey! We need some serious background on the country! There were forecasts of upheaval in the Balkans. An uprising in northeastern Albania, which some people called Outer Albania and others called Kosovo, had just been put down. Was there any connection between that rebellion and the event that had just taken place inside the country?

On one of the files, some exasperated hand had inked a red circle around the words "Are there six million Albanians, or only one million?" and added an exclamation mark to the question. Then scrawled his own exclamation: "Unbelievable!" In the view of the unnamed annotator, such hazy reporting, such imprecision, boggled the mind. Lower down the page, an identical question mark stood next to the query "Muslims or Christians?" A pencilled note in the margin added, "If there are not just a million Albanians, and if they are not all Muslims, as the Yugoslavs assert, but six times as many, that's to say roughly the same size as other Balkan peoples, and if they're not just Muslim but split three ways between Catholicism, Orthodoxy and Islam, then the geopolitical picture we have of the whole peninsula will probably have to be turned completely upside down."

A transatlantic intelligence agency was the first to realise not only that its espionage operation in Albania was completely outdated, but that a significant number of its agents, most of whom were getting on in years, had gone over to the Albanian *Sigurimi*. That was presumably why the news from the country following the death of the Successor was so disconcerting.

Nonetheless, the western cemetery of the capital was the scene of the burial of the deceased, which took place in a biting December wind. Members of the family were in attendance, together with a couple of dozen high-ranking state officials. There were some government ministers and the heads of a number of institutions, among them the white-maned president of the Academy of Sciences. Soldiers and other officials bore wreaths. The funeral oration was pronounced by the dead man's son. As he reached his final words — "Father, may you rest in peace" — his voice cracked. No salute was fired, no funeral march played. Suicide was still, very obviously, a mortal stain.

The December night swallowed the hills that surround Tirana one after the other, as if it was in a hurry to get the day over with. Two solitary soldiers in arms standing guard at the head and the foot of the newly filled grave of the Successor appeared to be all alone in the civilian necropolis. About a hundred feet away in the dark, other people not in uniform slunk behind the hedge, on the look out.

4

The relief that a newly buried corpse brings to the living did not fail to materialise. Not to mention that, for reasons readily imagined, it was more profound than ever before.

The days of anxiety gave way to unseasonable quiet. Milder weather altered the December skies and drained off what had been tormenting the population, or at least made it seem less terrifying. Even the underlying question — deciding whether it had been suicide or murder — no longer had the same weight, since the Successor had taken the answer with him to the grave.

Now they were free of the bottomless dread that the deceased had exuded, now that the man's corpse had finally disappeared into the dark, people found it easier to grasp all that had happened in the course of that long-drawn-out autumn. The event and its un-folding were now cast in a very different light.

It had all begun with the first days of September. On their return from holiday, city-dwellers found the capital buzzing with rumours of the kind that in the past might have been called scandals. The Successor had just promised the hand of his only daughter to a suitor. In addition, he'd just moved into his new resi-dence, a building project that had attracted a great deal of interest and attention in Tirana. In fact, what was referred to as the "new residency" was the same villa he'd been living in for years, but it had been re-modelled with such skill that over the course of the summer it had been transformed beyond recognition. Despite innumerable campaigns to eradicate supersti-tions, the old saw that "new houses bring new curses" seemed to be coming true as the autumn set in. It was never known whether the Successor believed in the saying or not, but there was unending gossip about his rushing to celebrate his daughter's engagement on the very day of the housewarming party. It looked as though, by taking this step, the Successor had wanted to force a blessing into his new house. In other words, he had tried to trick fate, or to defy it.

Everybody responded to the summons: family members and members of the government, the relatives of the putative son-in-law, and of course the young man himself, who had played the guitar, as well as the architect who had designed the new home, and who, having become roaring drunk, began to weep. Some people laughed and some cried as they wandered around a house lit by the glint of crystal and camera flashes. But before the party lights went out, and as the Guide (whose attendance and good wishes had constituted the high point of the soirée) was on his way back to his own residence on foot, an icy draught coming out of nowhere suddenly seemed to chill all who were still there.

Had he heard some unexpected news during the brief walk from the house of the Successor to his own? Had it been handed to him en route, as he plodded with short strides, weighed down by his black coat — or had he found it on the doorstep as he reached home? Nobody ever knew. On the other hand, it is true that from that point on, the first rumours of ill omen began to circulate: namely, that the Successor had made a political error in agreeing to the engagement. Despite the fact that the Party granted the future bridegroom's father, the famous seismologist Besim Dakli, permission to give an occasional lecture at the university, the Dakli clan still belonged to the ancien régime. You could have turned a blind eye if the bride had been the daughter of a second-rank official, but there was no way you could pass over such an issue where the Successor was concerned.

The dread question, which was expressed less in words than through pregnant glances and oblique allusions, related to the fact that the alliance between the family of the Successor and the Dakli clan had been made public at least two weeks before the Guide had paid his visit. It could thus be inferred that his attendance at the party, and the expression of his good wishes, signified his approval of said engagement. That is, moreover, the probable reason why that unforgettable day had been so exceptionally joyous. Nonetheless, as soon as the Guide had left the house, something strange happened. Was it a last and unexpected discovery about the Daklis? A piece of information coming from who knows where, or maybe from far away, about some disturbing fact that two weeks of intense investigation by every branch of the service about every imaginable dimension of the Dakli case had failed to turn up until then?

As often happens to people who stave off asking dangerous questions by showing uncommon interest in matters they believe much safer, gossipers kept on circling back to the issue of whether or not what was forbidden to others might be permitted the Successor. Most people thought not, and they ventured to recall numerous instances where ill-considered marriages had brought families, and even whole clans, to sorry ends. But there were some people who thought differently. The Successor had done so much for the country, he had followed the Guide every step of the way with such touching steadfastness through the most horrible turns of fate, that he surely deserved an exception to be made for him. What's more, they said, maybe this case in particular would set the wheels of change in motion. It was hard luck for people who'd already come unstuck, but that shouldn't stop the rest of us from profiting from new rules. That's just our point, the naysayers insisted, that's how rot sets in. No good can come of setting a bad example to others.

This sort of conversation was stopped in its tracks by the news that the engagement had been broken off. Each party had finally realised to what extent the whole thing had been worse than a mistake. It wasn't a prospective marriage, it was mortal venom. But poison would have tasted sweet compared to the true horror of such an event! An event that would have plunged Albania into everlasting sorrow. For it would have signified a relaxation of the class struggle, and that would have borne a blow to the very heart of what had been the country's pride for more than forty years. The country's very Constitution, the foundation of its victories and its fame, rested solely on the principle of *ever greater firmness*, of *never letting up*! Other countries, enemy countries, had betrayed Albania one by one, and their wrongdoing had unfailingly started that way — with a loosening of the reins. Whereas here, in our country . . . heaven grant that the Successor had suffered only a passing weakness! That's what it must have been, in all probability. That the engagement had been broken off so quickly spoke volumes about the depth of the man's repentance. It was no mere trifle to take back your given word in a matter of marriage. In full sight of the entire nation, he had had to eat his shame on a dry crust, as people say in these parts. No betrothal had been abjured in the land for a thousand years. People may have slaughtered each other, may have flayed each other alive, but not once had a wedding been postponed, let alone cancelled! But he had done it! And by so doing he had shown that obedience to the Party and to the *Prijs* — the Guide — ruled his heart. That showed you what sort of a fellow he was! You don't get to be Successor for nothing, now do you?

5

Like all bad news, the report of the broken engagement got around much faster than its formal announcement. Convinced that the crisis was a thing of the past, most people liked to think that the incident, far from weakening the nation's moral fibre, had in fact strengthened it. The country and its Guide had shown just how steadfast they were in a storm of whatever magnitude. Just as they had done during the squabble with the Yugoslavs. As they did later on, with the Russians. And, of course, with the Chinese.

As tension declined, so interest in the sentimental details of the end of the affair grew. Though whispered, stories were passed on by word of mouth almost everywhere. No more phone calls between the two youngsters. The young man and his father, Besim Dakli, standing at the Successor's front door, wrapped in heavy winter coats, waiting to find out what would happen. The girl in despair, who had shut herself in her room and stopped eating. The poor boy drowning his sorrow by strumming his guitar, for which he'd written a new song that began:

> And so that is how
> They tore us apart . . .

In Albania, the majority of public holidays occur in the autumn, which meant that the Successor had no chance of keeping himself out of the way of television cameras. Awkward as that was for him, there was no way he could avoid thousands of eyes studying his face on screen, searching for a clue to the real truth. Some thought he looked more grumpy than usual; others thought on the contrary that he looked calmer. Both interpretations were obviously worrying, but the latter seemed the more ominous, since it implied that the Successor was feigning indifference.

What had begun as mere curiosity took on a

tragic hue at the National Day parade, where the Guide and the Successor stood side by side on the platform. In contrast to previous occasions, when the two had been seen smiling and chatting with each other, this year the Guide stood stock-still. Not only did he not utter a word to the Successor, but, as if to make his scorn doubly clear, he turned twice to say something to the person standing on his other side — the minister of the interior.

From one end of the country to the other, people were dumbfounded by what they saw happening before their eyes. The benighted engagement had long been broken off, but no reward, not even a sign of clemency, had yet been granted the Successor for the action he had taken. On the contrary, everything seemed to suggest that the Guide was only growing angrier.

It was the first time people had seen what almost amounted to a public display of things that in the old days could have had you convicted of malicious gossip seeking to undermine Party unity. The militant Party members were racked with worry. They would rise at dawn after sleepless nights, with bloodshot eyes, aching muscles, and coated tongues, turn to their greying wives and share with them what could not be

broached in any bar: Could a forty-year-old comrade-
ship be scrapped just like that?

The optimists among them looked forward to the
next parade, hoping that, if things would not be completely resolved by then, at least some slight improve-
ment might be visible. And when the next parade day
came, and not only had nothing mended, but the chill
was even icier, they felt a great weight on their chest
and, sighing with anxiety, barely managed to articu-
late the words "Woe betide us!"

Towards the end of November, a tentative rumour had it that the whole business would come to an
end at the winter break. Oddly enough, it gained
greater acceptance than other stories, perhaps because
it invoked the calendar and the natural cycle of the
seasons. The red banners and bunting on the stands,
the speeches and brass bands broadcast by the city-
wide loudspeaker system, would give way to whistling
winds, to blankets of fog, and to the rumble of thunder, which had not changed in a thousand years.

And if the first week of December had always
been labeled "taciturn", this year it seemed doubly,
triply speechless. It was this silence that was broken by
the gunshot that put an end to the life of the Successor.
A fully muffled shot, moreover, a shot not heard outside

the residence, or even inside its walls. As if the gun had been fired from beyond the grave.

6

The Albania files had come to give their users such troubles that, even if they did not admit it to themselves, their desire to see the short-term upheaval in the country settle down, and to see those files once again gathering dust, became almost noticeable.

Alas, for the time being, there was no point even dreaming of such a thing. On the contrary, those brown folders got heavier by the day. Everyone realised that the material piling up inside them was contradictory and incoherent, to such a degree that even the most persistent analysts ended up making the same gesture of despair as everyone else and declaring, with arms thrown wide: The only way you can get a grip on a place overcome by paranoia is by becoming a little paranoid yourself.

Their superiors in the agencies seemed to think otherwise. They scribbled spindly question marks over words and phrases like "hereditary Balkan lunacy", "whim", "delusion", "symptomatic brain damage from iodine deficiency", and so forth. A leader's envy of his successor, envy taken to the point of murdering him, was such a common event in every place and period that it could not itself provide a key to understanding the Balkan malady. You could call to mind some of the customs of Albanian mountain tribes — for instance, their male beauty contests that were often followed by the killing of the winner, for reasons of envy, obviously — if you were writing a literary essay, but definitely not if you were trying to present a serious political analysis. And if you did, it would come down to saying that the whole history of the peninsula was no more than a working out of the old legend about the mirror on the wall: "Mirror, mirror on the wall, who is the fairest one of all . . ."

The analysts ended up coming back to the main questions, after wearing themselves out in the pursuit of the puzzling issues raised by the beauty contests in the northern highlands — which could be understood either as a symptom of almost prehistoric male vanity, or as an indulgence of homosexuality by Albanian common law, which in other respects was so harsh.

Responding to repeated comments that it was time to be a bit more serious, the specialists on the Balkan desk came back once again to their other hypothesis, the one marked with a huge question mark: Is the country changing its political line? Obviously, the first thing that occurred to them was to make a connection between the murder of the Successor and some preceding attempt by him to deviate from orthodoxy. Unfortunately, the huge mass of intelligence now reaching them contained not the slightest, not the tiniest, sign that the Successor had ever tried to introduce the minutest change in the political line of the Albanian regime.

Though it was true that marriage with a member of an ancien régime family could be interpreted in Albania as a sign of relaxation of the class struggle, aside from this fact the Successor was the last person who could be accused of slackness in class warfare. Throughout his long career, he had been a hard-liner at every turn, never a moderate. He had taken on that role long before, and for years people had suspected that when the Guide wanted to impose harsh measures, he first sent the Successor out ahead of him as a kind of herald. Then, if the measure once taken seemed excessive, the Successor was ready and willing to take the blame, allowing the Guide to play the role of moderator.

This time, everything had happened backwards.

The specialists were dying to put the whole thing down to a classical case of Albanian eccentricity but regrettably had to refrain, as they swung back to the second hypothesis, namely, that the reason for the crisis lay in the recent disturbances in Kosovo.

The whole preceding year had been marked by gloomy forecasts. Kosovo was going to be the next earthquake, it was a coming tornado, a horror waiting to happen in the Balkans. Everywhere, heads would roll as a result of the rebellion — that was only logical, but it was nowhere more logical than in Albania. But in what manner was the fate of the Successor connected to the uprising? The rumours on that topic became ever more confused. The Yugoslavs had been the first to sow the suspicion of murder, but, as if regretting having said too much, they had now fallen silent. Did they really know nothing, or were they just pretending?

One of the analysts, at his wits end because neither of the geopolitical explanations really stood up, thus went back to the discarded hypothesis that his colleagues had dubbed the "mirror on the wall" theory. Presumably in order to make it more credible, he had recourse to what was in those days the sine qua non of most conflict analyses, namely oil. Though his paper was backed up with all sorts of figures on Albania's petroleum output since the 1930s and geological charts of the oil-bearing areas — it even included a rundown on the squabble between British Petroleum and the Italian Agip company in 1938 — it was dismissed as "ridiculous". The latter epithet might well not have been used had the analyst not added, by way of conclusion, that it could hardly be a coincidence that the Successor's daughter's unfortunate putative ex-father-in-law was a seismologist, a profession that one way or another related to surveying for oil . . .

As a consequence of the failure of his attempt to pinpoint, at six thousand feet beneath the surface, the causes of the broken engagement and the suicide, the analyst, as might be expected, threw in the towel. In accordance with his recently acquired custom of adding long supplementary notes to everything he wrote, he accompanied his request for early retirement with a long account of the state of his health that winter, which was backed up by two medical certificates one of which was headed "impotence".

His colleagues had no intention of following suit, though that did not stop them dreaming of one day having the Albania files removed from their purview. Any other desk would be better, even one with an

abysmal reputation, like the Israeli-Palestinian con-
frontation, or some African countries with frontiers
that were less a reflection of political changes than of
the desert winds, as they had been centuries earlier.

They sighed deeply, cursing that "basket case of a
country", and went back to the unyielding file,
attempting to start over as simply as possible.

Murder or suicide? If a murder, who was the cul-
prit? For what motive? Most of the material that had
been collected continued to point to the very highly
placed official whose silhouette had been seen slipping into the Successor's residence in the course of the
fateful night. Some reports even went so far as to give
a name to the person suspected of being that shadow:
Adrian Hasobeu, the minister of the interior. He had
just left that job to go up a further rung in the hierarchy.
All intelligence forecasts made him the Successor's
most likely replacement.

A host of other details combined with the fleet-
ing shadow to make the fog even murkier. The
Successor's request to be awakened at eight; his wife
sleeping like a log; the tang of gunpowder that had
greeted her when she opened the door on the stroke of
eight. All those comings and goings in the *Bllok*
throughout the night. The wind and the rain that

kept changing direction. Two men had apparently been seen from the outside (perhaps by one of the sentries) going up or down the staircase of the residence. Thanks to a flash of lightning, they had been glimpsed on the first-floor veranda propping the Successor up like a tailor's dummy.

Was he still alive when they took him back up — or down? Had he fainted? Was he wounded? Or dead? Were they taking him to the basement or to the morgue? To have him made up to look presentable, perhaps? Or to move the wound, by stopping up the bullet hole, for instance, and replacing it with another? However, there was a secret passageway in the basement that nobody knew about . . .

All these ingredients churned unrelentingly in sombre spirals moving now slower, now faster, swirling this way and that, in whorls that came and went, disappeared and reappeared, and finally sank out of sight. But in every variant of the mix, the ingredients themselves remained irreducible and in the end came to resemble shards of glass, or a substance that was simultaneously the stock and the fermenting agent without which no mystery could have risen.

Intelligence analysts were near the end of their tether as they struggled over the Albania files. It was the first time they had switched from one theory to another with such abandon. For instance, the first idea that occurred to anyone looking at the information about the silhouette was that it belonged to the Successor's assassin. But you only had to look at things in their proper order to realise that such a deduction was far from safe. Even assuming that the said silhouette (and assuming it was Adrian Hasobeu's) had got into the residence, how could you be sure of the purpose of the late-night visit? Was he on his way to commit murder, or to push the Successor to kill himself? But what if instead of either of these he had been aiming to persuade the Successor not to pull the trigger, seeing that at the Politburo meeting scheduled for the next day he was going to be forgiven?

To cap it all, there was the secret passageway mentioned by some of the investigators, which made everything even more impenetrable.

Here and there in the paperwork you came across notes in telegraphese, such as: "Need know if architect villa still alive." Didn't the pharaohs kill the architect the moment a pyramid was completed?

There was something pyramid-like about the whole business. Walls suddenly sprang up all around and blocked the slightest progress. The main chamber of the pyramid, where the most precious secret was kept, was locked from the inside. The same timeless principle was probably involved in the affair of the Successor.

The analogy was reassuring, in a way. The mysteries of the pyramids had not been completely solved in four thousand years. So why should intelligence analysts be in so much of a hurry in this case?

Taking advantage of all this haziness, clairvoyants — who had been making a comeback in recent times, after nearly fifty years' absence from the field of state secrets — tried to intervene. But once contact was established with the spirit of the Successor, what could be gleaned from him was so obscure and undecipherable that, one after the other, the clairvoyants all ended up admitting defeat.

Oddly enough, Albania seemed to have sunk into never-ending silence. Over the border, the other Albania, "Outer" Albania, lay still and stiff under the winter sky, as if it had been laid low by a stroke. The same December sky arched over them, but it was a sky of such desolation that it seemed to be nursing two winters, not just one, two winters that were pacing up and down and howling like wolves.

TWO

THE AUTOPSY

1

Whatever was that feeling of joy, which seemed like nothing on earth? With a glass of champagne in her hand, Suzana sauntered among the guests as if she was walking on air. The great house, uninhabited since her father's suicide, was once more full of people, light, and sound, just like it used to be. Nobody expressed surprise, moreover, just as nobody asked how the impossible had happened or why things had gone back to the way they were. Quite a few of the guests were unfamiliar, but that also did not seem surprising. Similarly, no one worried about how some of the bulbs in the chandeliers had failed to come on — having burned out from long disuse. For the second time, she heard someone saying, "What's gone is gone and never comes back", and then she set about looking for her father. Although he was the overall focus of attention, he was standing a little to the side, with a thin smile on his face that seemed to express some mild displeasure that would not be hard to dissipate. Suzana's eyes lighted immediately on the white bandage that could be seen through her father's shirt, presumably to protect the wound while it was healing. She put down her glass of champagne before going up to him and saying simply, "Papa, how are you feeling?" At that very moment she remembered she had still not seen Genc, her fiancé, among the guests, and almost shouted: How is it possible that he is the only one not to have come?

Albeit silent, the shout was what must have awakened her. As on the last occasion when she had had the same dream, Suzana burst into tears. She must have been weeping in her sleep as well, since the pillow was damp. She was holding it tightly to her face in the hope of going back to sleep when she thought she heard sounds. She raised her head to listen, and realised that her ears had not deceived her. There were people coming and going in the house.

Her eyes wandered toward the window. Then she

switched on the light and looked at her watch. It was six-thirty in the morning, but the sky behind the curtains was still dark.

The noises resumed. They were not her mother's footsteps, nor those of her brother, who habitually locked the bathroom door at that hour. They were something different. Apprehension lay like a lead weight on her chest, yet deeper down she felt no fear at all, but a kind of joy, as if she was still inside her dream.

She got up in a state of bewilderment and went to the door. Before turning the handle, she stood stock-still, to listen for voices.

The landing was quiet, but muffled sounds of speech and feet rose from below. Her mother's and brother's bedroom doors were shut. She went over to the railing and looked down into the hall. The lights had been switched on in the dining room and the grand salon, the room where her dream had taken place.

Her heart raced. Since her father's suicide, irrespective of anyone's wishes, it had been forbidden to enter that room, which had been formally sealed by order of the Ministry of the Interior.

She turned her head slowly to look once more

at the doors of the bedrooms where her mother and brother slept, and then, in a growing panic, she stared at the other door on the landing, the door to her father's room. A razor-thin strip of light shone from beneath. Every part of her body — her lungs, her eyes, her hair — screamed in unison: Papa! It was the same strip of light she had watched until two in the morning during the fatal night. She told herself she must still be dreaming, as she had not collapsed instantly like someone struck by lightning. With measured step, fearing she might wake herself up and thus lose this second chance of seeing her father come back, she moved towards the door. Yes, she must be asleep, or else out of her mind, since she felt that she would see her father again in the very bedroom where she had seen him dead, with a hole in his bloodstained shirt.

One more step, then another. Don't give up now, she told herself. In any case, you're done for.

At that moment the door swung open. A stranger rushed out. He was holding something black that looked like an old kind of camera. He looked the young woman up and down, somewhat surprised, and then, without uttering a word, raced down the stairs two at a time.

From the other side of the bedroom door that

the stranger had left ajar came the sound of an exasperated man. Suzana managed to make out the word "autopsy".

What next? That would really be the last straw if, after all the horror, they were now going to conduct an autopsy on the spot using an obsolete instrument in the shape of a camera.

Suzana put a hand to her forehead. It was probably just the continuation of her dream. Or did she mean hallucination?

Voices rose in the bedroom once more. A snatch of speech caught her ear: ". . . failing to carry out an autopsy was a scandalous omission!"

The door opened wide. His face crimson with anger, a man she thought she recognised as the new minister of the interior hurried out. Of his two escorts she recognised only one — the architect of the residence, the only one of them to have been in her recent dream.

The minister stared at her with some surprise. He stopped in his tracks to say, "Good morning!" then added, "Did we wake you up?"

The young woman hardly knew what to say.

The architect greeted her with a gentle nod of his head.

"We are making some inquiries," the minister said before moving toward the staircase.

The other two followed in his footsteps. As they went down the stairs, Suzana once again heard the words "autopsy" and "scandal".

The minister had sounded and looked very friendly.

She felt as if she was regaining her senses. They had apparently come before dawn to proceed with their inquiries. The day after Father's death they had given close family members permission to go on living in part of the residence but not to enter the closed rooms and areas designated by red sealing wax. From time to time they would come to carry out various checks. They had the keys.

That's what they had said, but they hadn't come. This morning was the first time they had shown their faces. So if Suzana had felt entitled to ask a single question, it would have been: What took you so long?

The young woman felt a wave of cold settle on her shoulders. Her feet took her to her mother's bed-room door. How in the world could she not be up, with all the commotion in the house?

She turned the handle carefully and pushed the door open.

"Mama," she said in a whisper, so as not to startle her. But her mother seemed to be sleeping like a log.

Suzana stood rigid on the threshold, not sure what to do. Incredible! she said inwardly. Her mother, who was in the habit of rising at first light, was still deep in the land of Nod. Just like the other time, on the night of December 14.

"Mama!" she said a second time.

It took the drowsy woman another minute to come to. You could see she was beginning to panic.

"What's the matter?" she snapped. "What's going on?"

"They've come to check . . . They're here, in Papa's bedroom, and downstairs as well, in the grand salon . . ."

Her mother's eyes bulged, but seemed to be blind.

"To check what? What for?"

"Their inquiries," the daughter replied. "The minister himself has come. He said they were going to do an autopsy."

The woman's hair, as much as her eyes, suggested distress. As if it was the last part of her to shake off sleep.

"What's all this nonsense about an autopsy? Why can't they just leave us alone?"

"They're going to do an autopsy," the daughter repeated. "They even said it was a scandal that one hasn't been done before. Mama," she added more gently, "I think it's not . . . not a bad idea."

"You do, do you? And what's not bad about it?" the older woman retorted, as she tried to cover her face with the pillow. It muffled the sound of her next words. "What's not bad about it? You're into autopsies now, are you?"

Suzana bit her lower lip. She was about to walk out, but changed her mind.

"I think it's a good sign . . . The inquiry itself is a good thing. You're aware there are suspicions that . . ."

"Hold your tongue!" the mother shouted. And after a moment she wailed, "Unhappy that we are! Misfortune will be upon us evermore!"

Suzana shook her head in despair, and left.

The landing was still shrouded in half-light. Voices from downstairs had a muffled sound. Outside, dawn was breaking.

She went back to her own room, shivering with the chill. All the same, she could not rid herself of a kind of good premonition. The minister's eyes had been so kindly. And especially his voice. He had given just as much an impression of firmness when speaking of the autopsy as he had of attentiveness when he turned to her and said, "Did we wake you up?"

So someone had not wanted an autopsy . . . somebody who might be held accountable . . . You avoid an autopsy when you have something to hide . . . In the present case, it wasn't hard to imagine what . . . Had the event really been a suicide, or had it been . . . had it been . . . murder? In circumstances of this kind, an autopsy was normally obligatory . . . All the more so when the deceased was so prominent. Therefore, someone had wanted to hide something . . . Whereas now, someone else wanted the secret out in the open . . . Someone who went so far as to call the cover-up a "scandal" . . .

My God, let it be so! Suzana implored. She wasn't even surprised anymore that she had invoked the forbidden name.

Truth would out in the end for all to see . . . The Party . . . as always . . . as ever . . . No, our comrade in arms, the trustworthy, the unforgettable . . . did not take his own life, as was first thought, but was murdered . . . perfidiously . . . by enemies of the Party . . . by saboteurs . . . by traitors . . .

She had already dreamed so many times of hearing these words from the mouth of the Guide standing on a red-draped platform or speaking on the radio or the television! But this was the first time they seemed to her to be within the range of possibilities. My God, let it happen! she prayed once more.

She was keeping her eyes shut in the hope that she would return to the dream she had been dreaming that morning and would discover its sequel. Such things had happened before, but rarely, so very rarely. And even when that did happen, there was never any correction. She tried to reconstruct it from memory, but she soon realised that, however hard she tried, she could not bring back its sweetness of tone any more than she could make pink clouds stay longer in the sky. The only thing she could still feel was the bitter taste of regret at the moment of waking. Maybe the reason she so much wanted to return to the dream — if only for a few seconds — was so she could wash away the regret. Except that she was no longer very sure what depressed her the more — that she had not managed to speak to her father, or that she had not had a thought for her fiancé until the very end . . .

2

"Let's do this again," the minister said in a casual, almost jovial tone of voice.

His words sounded less like those of a senior official in charge of a crucial autopsy, the most important to have taken place in the history of the Communist State of Albania and maybe in all Albanian history, than like someone saying goodbye to old friends after a sumptuous meal in one of the restaurants in the hills around Tirana's artificial lake. "The fish is really great here. Let's do this again, okay?"

Is this case going to be tied up or not?

Petrit Gjadri, the forensic pathologist, strode along the Grand Boulevard toward the Hotel Dajti, thinking all the while about the minister's remark, which grew a tad more inconceivable with every step he took.

The architect drank in the minister's words with feverish eyes that could have signified either pathological inquisitiveness or prurient pleasure — the kind of look that spreads like wildfire at the circus or at a fistfight in the market, when spectators or passersby rub their hands as if to say: Let's see how this turns out!

Are they both blind, or are they just pretending? the doctor had wondered as he watched them trading jokes like a couple of youngsters.

As for himself, he recalled quite clearly when he had been officially notified that he would be required to undertake an autopsy of prime importance. On the body of the Successor.

He had gone deaf for a brief instant. The whole universe had gone silent. Inside him, everything stopped — his heartbeat, his brain, his breathing. Then, as those functions gradually returned, a thought slowly formed in his mind: so that's how we'll put an end to this business.

"This business" was his own life.

After an autopsy of this kind, the continued existence of the person who carried it out seemed as improbable as evidence of life on the face of the moon.

In the oppressive silence, broken only by the minister giving instructions, the forensic pathologist, involuntarily as it were, looked back on his career with a strange sense of distance . . . He had lived an honest life, insofar as that was possible, and it had certainly not been easy, given the risky nature of the profession he pursued. He had always been vulnerable to attack on account of his "semi-bourgeois" family background, but he had escaped the campaign to unmask and denounce the "so-called intellectual circle of the Tirana doctors" — accused of denigrating Soviet life — as he had fortunately only been a student at the time. After that first stroke of luck, he had managed to steer clear of being identified with another group, a coalition of teachers and students who stood accused of making jokes about China's barefoot doctors, at the time of his country's idyll with Peking.

The minister's words were clear and unemotional, pregnant with ominous promises. One had failed to carry out a procedure that it was obligatory be made on any citizen, and even more so on the Successor: an autopsy.

The doctor tried to concentrate, but he felt as if that was only muddling his mind even more.

So the autopsy would be done, the minister went on, despite the delay. The truth must come out, irrespective of whether it was to any particular person's taste. The minister's eyes sparkled with sincere indignation.

At the meeting over the Chinese, sincerity was precisely what had been lacking in the delegates from the Party Committee. They had feigned outrage by pounding the tabletop and making their voices quaver, but it was manifest that their hearts were as cold as damp kindling. All the same, the terror that cold fury can arouse is no less fearful than others — the sort that is accompanied by oohs and aahs. But at the end of the meeting, when they were waiting in petrified fear for the sentences to be declared, the first rumours of the break with Peking began to circulate, and the campaign was stopped in its tracks, as if by magic.

Everything would be done by the rules, the minister went on with unchanging indignation. Apart from the autopsy, there would be a reenactment. A shot would be fired in the bedroom with the weapon that the victim had used. They would then verify whether the noise could be heard outside. In the garden, where the residence's guards were on duty. On the landing. In the bedrooms where the other family members were sleeping. Everything would be carefully taken down. They would pick a stormy night with weather similar to that of December 14. Shots would be fired with a silencer, then without one.

The doctor's eyes met the architect's, without meaning to. What self-destroyer had ever fitted a silencer to the gun he was going to use? But instead of a glimmer of disbelief, what shone in the architect's eyes was the same feverish euphoria as before.

Did he really understand nothing, or was that just a way of protecting himself?

"We'll begin with the test with the silencer on," the minister repeated, but, as if he could read the doctor's thoughts, he added immediately, "I'm sure I don't need to remind you that this whole . . . business is strictly confidential."

He was on the verge of saying explicitly that at the end of the story the Successor's death would be shown to have been murder, that the man would be declared a Martyr of the Revolution, and that all the suspicions that had darkened his name like so many leaden clouds would be blown away there and then. That fact would lead directly to the punishment of those who had brought the Successor down.

"Be that as it may," the minister went on as he glanced at the doctor with just an ounce of affection, "the key to the whole business is the autopsy."

Of course it is, Petit Gjadri thought.

In his heart of hearts, he had always known that one day or another an autopsy would be his undoing.

Do you think your words fill me with joy? he responded inwardly to the minister's remarks.

Obviously he knew what the score was. In times like these, any given autopsy could be interpreted and

43

then reinterpreted on a whim or a change of wind. The results might be appropriate to the general climate on this day, and not at all acceptable the day after. Barely a few weeks ago, Kano Zhbira, a former member of the Politburo who had committed suicide quite a few years back, had been exhumed from the Martyrs of the Motherland Cemetery. It was his third unearthing! Every tack and turn in the political line exercised its primary effect on human remains, not on the national economy. Zhbira's posthumous rheumatism — *rheumatismus post mortem*, a condition that does not yet afflict us — was a better indicator of political change than any analyst's prediction. Immediately after his suicide (together with rumours that it had been murder, of course) he had been buried with full honours in the Martyrs' Cemetery. Shortly thereafter, he had been hauled up at the request of the Yugoslavs and transferred to Tirana's municipal graveyard, signs of anti-Yugoslavianism having been detected in his file. A year later, after the break with Yugoslavia, he was dug up again so as to be put back in his original tomb in the national cemetery — as a herald of anti-Yugoslavianism. His third and most recent unburying, which took his body to the municipal graveyard once again, had been done almost on the sly, but no one yet knew why.

Cawing from above made the doctor raise his eyes. He smiled to himself, thinking that the Greeks must have been quite near the mark in divining political fortunes from patterns made by flocks of birds.

They were all washed up, the three of them, that was for sure. Including the minister, who headed their little group. But like the architect, he did not seem to have grasped the fact, unless the pair of them were putting on an act. Instead, they seemed to find the case entertaining; far from hiding this, they went in for larks and japes as if they were not a government minister and a senior architect but a couple of merry-makers. When it was over, before parting, they had a few words in private, then vanished together into the basement of the residence.

The doctor immediately put them out of his mind in order to concentrate his thoughts on the autopsy. That it was, at the very least, an autopsy of the first magnitude was not much consolation to him, but on the other hand he could have ended up like his colleague Ndré Pjetergega. A Gypsy from Brraka had lain in wait for him behind his door and, with a shout of,

"Doctor? Bastard! Are you the one who said my daughter was pregnant?" he had beaten him to death.

The yellowing leaves in the park on the other side of the Grand Boulevard made him sigh. God knows why, but the refrain of an old homosexual lament, which he'd heard years before in Shkodër, kept running through his mind:

> They say two candles were lit
> At the Vizier's yesterday.
> Holy Virgin, for Sulçabeg we pray:
> His throat a razor has slit.

In the corridor of the Successor's residence, the doctor was suddenly seized by the vision of the young woman in a nightdress revealing the shape of her delicate, quivering limbs. It was her engagement, it was she herself who lay at the root of her father's tragedy. And therefore at the root of a tragedy that would be their common lot.

As he was stepping inside the Hotel Dajti, a question began to form unobtrusively and gradually in his mind. Why had he, Petrit Gjadri, been chosen to perform this prestigious autopsy? But henceforth he should not try to answer that or any other question.

He was under a stay of execution, and he had to try to use the time remaining to good effect. The coffee he was going to enjoy in a hotel set aside for the exclusive use of foreigners and members of the nomenklatura — a place he would have dared to enter previously only in quite exceptional circumstances — would be just a foretaste of the higher serenity that was slowly spreading through his being. The kind of freedom that humans call "the peace of the grave", without really appreciating it insofar as they usually experience it only as they die, had, in this particular case, become available to him a little ahead of time.

He strode purposefully toward a table without even glancing at the customers at the bar. With an icy stare he turned to the waiter and asked almost casually for a double shot.

3

Six hundred feet away, the architect was hurrying home, with his chin buried in the upturned collar of his coat. His wife had been more adamant than ever: "As soon as you're done, you come straight back. No café, no club, no 'just ran into whatsisname'. Is that clear? I'll be waiting for you in fear and trembling. Can't you imagine? Our lives, the lives of our children, everything depends on what happens today, doesn't it?"

The architect looked at his watch. After the forensic pathologist had left the room, as he himself was about to bid the minister goodbye with a handshake, the politician had whispered to him, "Stay a while longer!"

Putting an arm around his shoulder, the way leaders do when wishing to indicate a degree of goodwill toward intellectuals, the minister asked almost in the same breath, "So what's this story about an underground passageway? . . ."

The architect lowered his eyelids, then shook his head as if to say: I don't know anything, it's the first I've heard of it. The minister kept on staring at him, but his eyes shone not so much with disbelief as with a kind of warmth. "So it was just boozers' idle gossip!" he exclaimed without hesitation, letting his anger show. "If the building's own architect isn't aware of it, how could they know about it?" He went on cursing gossipmongers for a while. Dogs, runts, incurable shiteaters . . . One of these days he would have them strung up by their balls.

To bring his litany of oaths to an end, and just as the architect was about to take his leave, the minister said, in the same conspiratorial whisper as before, "What say we take a quick trip into the basement, just to give it the once-over?"

The architect felt overcome by dizziness. The floor seemed to be opening up beneath his feet.

A bodyguard went ahead of them. The architect began to give brief explanations. "This passageway gives onto a second exit into the garden. The door cannot be opened from the outside, only from the inside, if you release several bolts. The other passage, the main one, leads to the air-raid shelter."

He was aware that his eyes were bulging, as if he was expecting at any moment to see someone's ghost looming out of the gloom.

"That way, no, there's nothing. This way, there's another wall. And over there . . . Hold tight! . . . Don't let me down! . . ." These words were not spoken to himself, but rather to a third wall that looked utterly normal and in every respect similar to the other walls. But he knew full well that its appearance was deceptive. Beneath the cladding lay an enigma whose existence was known to very few. That mystery was another door.

Nothing could have been more terrifying to the architect than the sight of that door. It had been fitted by someone else, without his having been informed; but that would not save him from having to answer for it if any problems arose. He would have preferred not to know, to have never known about it, but bad luck had deemed otherwise. A few days before completion of the remodelling, when at the request of the son of the Successor he went down into the basement to check whether the air-raid shelter was sufficiently well soundproofed to keep the racket of a night club from seeping out, the son pointed to an almost unnoticeable door and said in an almost jocular tone, "And there's the door, which according to what people suspect, leads all the way to the basement of the house of *Himself* . . ." Himself was the Guide. Taken aback when he realised the architect knew nothing about it, the young man didn't try to hide his distress at having let out the secret. Then he begged the architect never to whisper a word of it to anyone. But that very evening, as he did with many things he would have done better to forget, the architect mentioned it to his wife. And she wept, as she always did, and through her tears, not once but a dozen times, she kept on saying, "And from now on you keep quiet about it! Forget that door!

Since nobody outside of the two households knows, you're not supposed to be in on it either. What's more, they kept it hidden from you, even though you're the architect in charge of the rebuilding. Which definitely means you should be the last to know."

When the Successor died, that door once again became an even gloomier issue between the architect and his wife. "Are you sure you never said anything about it? Are you sure you never will say a word?" "Never, ever," he swore, "not even to my own grave." "Especially now," she said. "Because people are going to be having the worst kinds of thoughts from now on: the underground passageway connected the two villas . . . and the murderers could have used it. Oh, it's going from bad to worse for us!"

That morning as he was getting ready to go out, his tearful wife had reminded him again, "Be careful about that door business! You're the architect. But you're not at fault in any way. Only one thing can bring your downfall: your having seen that door."

Throughout the inspection of the Successor's residence, the architect kept repeating in his mind: Thank you, Lord, it's nearly over, this torture will soon be finished! But as luck would have it, at the very last moment, just as he was about to be on his way, the minister came out with that "What say we take a quick trip into the basement?" — and the evil trap snapped shut. An invitation to step downstairs into hell would not have been any more frightening to him.

The architect realised he had reached the building where he lived. His wife must be worrying herself sick in the meantime. He ran up the stairs. The door of his apartment opened the very moment he put his finger on the bell. His wife was actually standing just behind, waiting for him and shaking like a leaf. He kissed her and put her head to his cheek. He spoke to her through her hair: "It's over, over at last," he kept on saying. She looked up and noticed how pale he was. "Come in and calm down . . ."

They went into the bedroom. He lay down on his back and resumed his sighing prayer: Lord, it's over at last! She sat at the head of the bed and stroked his hair as he told the tale. He was very precise when he drew up plans for buildings, but a complete muddle when it came to words. When he got to the point where they had gone down the steps to the basement, his wife grasped his wrists. An old Muslim prayer for the dead came back to her: Be not afraid now that you must cross the darkness all alone . . .

So he had followed the minister's steps down the stairs, alert for the moment when the door would appear. But all of a sudden, in its stead and place, they had come upon a smooth-clad wall. The smell of plaster and new cement meant that the surfacing had been done very recently. "Two or three days ago, definitely not more than that. But for me it was the most beautiful finish in the whole wide world. Blessed wall! I thought. Wall of my hopes and prayers! I wanted to bow down to it like a Jew at the Western Wall. I wanted to weep and to chant. I don't know how I contained myself. The minister definitely had his eye on me. He was testing me, that much was obvious. What he was going to put in his report flashed through my head: 'The architect, when confronted with the wall, displayed no surprise; likewise when I mentioned the underground passageway to him.'"

His wife went on stroking his hair. "It's over, thank the Lord, it's over," she said from time to time. "Now it's shut for good . . ." "As far as we're concerned, yes indeed," he replied. "From our point of view the door is done for, but not for whoever installed it in the first place. Those poor guys must be shaking in their boots, if they've not been taken care of already."

She felt that her husband was getting ready to tell her something else, but was still unsure.

"Have a nap," she suggested. "Do you want me to lie down with you?"

"Come here, darling."

She took off her clothes and snuggled up to him. "Sleep, my dear, relax," she whispered in his ear. But his mind did not seem to be at rest. He clearly wanted to say something else.

"Is anything wrong?" she asked after a while.

He grunted. "Well, yes, there is something . . . that I just can't keep to myself."

His wife stiffened. "But you did tell me everything, didn't you?" she said sweetly and softly. "Besides all that, nothing else really matters. Now get some sleep!"

"No," the architect said. "It's better to bring it all up. That way it'll be off my chest . . . That door . . ."

His wife heard herself screaming out loud, "That damn door again! But you said it had been walled up! Shut up for all eternity . . ."

"That's the literal truth. Don't get excited, it's about something else. One day . . ."

The woman gripped his hand as all of a sudden her mind went back to the words of the old Muslim prayer.

He told her everything, in stark, cold, and unusually precise terms. One day, not long after the Successor's son had revealed the existence of the door, he had gone back down to the basement. His own accursed curiosity had driven him to it. So he had gone back down and looked for the door in the dingy gloom. He spent a while going over it with his hands, like a blind man, until he was sure of what he had half guessed already. *That* door could be opened from only one side — from *his* side. On that other side, there had to be bolts and locks, because on this side, the Successor's side, there was absolutely nothing!

"I don't understand," his wife butted in. "Is that all there is to your mystery?"

The architect smiled sourly. How could she not understand? The greatest mysteries are like child's play. The Guide and his people could get into the Successor's place whenever they wanted. Be it at dawn or on the stroke of midnight. But the Successor could not. Worse still: the Successor had no way of preventing the door from being opened. He wasn't supposed to. He didn't have the right to. Most likely that was what the agreement between them said.

At last the penny dropped. For a moment she was dumbstruck. "So the murderers could have gone that

55

way at their leisure . . . ?" she finally managed to artic-
ulate. "Do you realise what a catastrophe you have just
unearthed, you poor man?"

"Of course I do," he replied. "That's why I didn't
mention it earlier. God be my witness of the torture I
endured to keep it secret. It would have been easier to
nurse a black hole in my heart. Now that I've told you,
I feel a burden has lifted from my chest."

His wife began stroking him again.

"My poor boy," she murmured.

"That door," the architect resumed, "had one-
way hinges, like the gates of the hereafter."

The woman put her arms around him. It was time
for them to forget. Now that he had spat out the poison, there was nothing for them to do except to swear
they would never speak of it again. Not even in a
wasteland where not a breath of life stirred. Because
even places like that could send an echo of such a
secret. Like in the story of the barber who one day cut
the hair of a lord of bygone days . . .

"Wasn't that aristocrat called Gjork Golem?" he
queried. "Tell me the story again, please."

So she began to tell the tale, like she used to,
speaking very quietly, as if she were humming a lull-
aby. With half-closed eyes, the architect imagined the

wasteland and the barber coming across it, his face drawn and weary. The secret he had discovered when cutting the lord's hair was too terrible even to think about. The lord's threat had been of the same order — enough to send shivers up and down your spine. "If you repeat a single word about what you discovered when you were cutting my hair, you wretch, your life will not be worth a penny." But the barber could not imagine anything strong enough to keep him from revealing what he had seen: two tiny horns right at the back of the lord's head, at the top of his nape. Which was why he was wandering over the desolate moor in winter looking for the remotest spot possible where he could relieve himself of it by speaking it out loud. He stopped at an abandoned well, hidden by a few reeds waving in the wind, and squatting over it he spoke these words:

> Hark my words else I'll hold my tongue
> Gjork Golem's eyes may be dull and blear
> But the back of his head is yet more drear
> There's two little horns where men have none . . .

Then he went back to his village, feeling much relieved, and believing that now he had got the secret out of himself it would no longer torment him at home or in the tavern. However, not long after, a passing herder stopped at the same place and cut a reed to make himself a pipe to play. He trimmed it deftly, as shepherds know how, then made the seven air holes, and finally put it to his lips to try it out. Imagine his surprise when, instead of playing the herder's usual tune, the reed pipe spoke this rhyme:

> Hark my words else I'll hold my tongue
> Gjork Golem's eyes may be dull and blear
> But the back of his head is yet more drear
> There's two little horns where men have none . . .

What an extraordinary story, he kept saying to himself, while his wife whispered in his ear that now he had spat out the poison he would feel calmer and wouldn't even think anymore about that accursed door. Anyway . . . anyway, if perchance, like the barber, he felt the urge to unburden himself to some well, he could use her own well. Had he not told her that it was darker and more mysterious than any other?

He did what she suggested. But from deep inside his wife's body, and although the sound was quite muffled, he could make out: "Hark my words . . . else I'll hold my tongue . . . one way only . . . is that door hung!"

Terror stopped him from laughing. Then their mutterings drowned in the one's then the other's groaning, until silence returned.

His wife thought he had dropped off to sleep, but then he started mumbling again. All over Tirana people who suspected the Successor's suicide of being a murder in disguise kept whispering the same question: who could have killed him? They were besieged with all kinds of surmises, but nobody had a clue who the real murderer could be.

"Go to sleep now," she insisted. "Forget all about it. You're exhausted."

"I will, I will, but I won't be able to sleep until I've got one last thing off my chest. It is the absolutely last thing, believe me! — and so utterly secret that there really can be nothing more."

"Oh no," moaned his wife. "I don't want to hear any more!"

"It really is the last, I promise you. The very last. Then there'll be nothing but calm water."

She seemed to acquiesce, as she said nothing more. He brought his lips close to her ear and then

blurted out, "The murderer, the man everyone is looking for but will never find, is . . . me!"

Only with great effort did the architect's wife
keep from bursting into tears.

"You think I've gone mad? You don't believe me?"

His eyes were cold and blank. She had never seen
them look like that before.

"So you too don't want to believe me," he continued flatly. His eyes were clouding over with anger,
whereas she felt as though the world were falling apart
irremediably.

She leaned over, kissed him tenderly, and whispered in his ear, "Of course I believe you, dearest. If
you didn't do it, then who else could have?"

He took her hand, brought it to his lips with grat-
itude, and promptly fell asleep.

She propped herself up on her elbow and gazed
for a long while at his emaciated face, on which a
strange mask of serenity seemed to have been laid.

4

The temperature in the Albanian capital had fallen to
an unexpected low. Many had not realised that it was

late March, or else had forgotten the old saying according to which the third month often asks its brother February to lend it three bitter days, to chill the bones of whoever offends it.

With their collars turned up to keep out the cold, the people who scurried along to the meetings they had been summoned to attend in one or another of the fourteen main halls in the city had other things to worry about. They knew they had to take part in meetings of great moment related to the death of the Successor, but they felt utterly unable to guess what else might lie in store.

Those same people had been astonished that morning when, in their various offices, they had slit open their envelope and seen on the invitation that the customary hierarchy of assembly rooms had been completely disregarded. The vice-minister's typist was to go to the Opera, generally thought to be the most prestigious of the venues, whereas the vice-minister himself had been summoned to a classroom in the Agricultural College, in which he had never before set foot. However, that was only the first surprise. Once they were at their respective meeting places, the participants found other causes for astonishment. Unlike all other occasions of this kind, no long table stood on the podium, there was no red tablecloth on it, and no flowers either. All they could see was a chair by a plain square table on which a tape recorder stood. Even that was nothing compared to the shock caused by the seating plan. Office workers, professors, truck drivers, greying female party activists, members of the Politburo, and government ministers silently suffered inner dramas as they checked, and checked again, the seat number printed on their invitation before they finally sat down beside each other. Some occasionally felt a sudden wave of joy at having such high officials sitting next to them, but these feelings of pride metamorphosed almost instantly into dread, for reasons no one could quite explain.

An hour and a half later, as they came out, people seemed as if they had been struck dumb. By means of the tape recorder, they had just heard the Guide's speech to the Politburo, the same speech that had been intended for the evening of December 13, in the presence of the Successor, which had had to be postponed, given the lateness of the hour, to the next day, December 14. And it was in the interval between the evening of the thirteenth and the dawn of the fourteenth that the Successor's suicide had occurred.

The Guide's speech began by making you think

that the Successor, aware that he stood to be attacked next morning, had lacked the courage to wait for the hour of his punishment and so anticipated it by taking his own life. But lo and behold, to everyone's surprise, the speech ended with the announcement of the Successor's pardon. That sufficed to reverse the sequence of events in people's imagination.

Thousands of the inhabitants of the capital felt the same disturbance, identical to what had been felt some time previously by Politburo members on the morning of December 14. In living memory, no one could recall such a brutal stop being put to the working of the clock. Because of this interruption, the twelve hours that had elapsed, most of them night hours topped with the beginning of sunrise, had been completely swallowed up. It had thus been a sudden Tuesday, though endowed with a secret dose of clemency that Monday had given it. The Guide's soft and at times almost liquid voice, coming close to a gurgle, cut through total silence. He addressed the Successor by his first name, as he had in the past: "And now, when you have had time to think again during the night, I am absolutely certain that when we gather again tomorrow in this same room, you will have an even clearer understanding of your mistake and you will at last be with us once again, with your comrades who love you, and as precious to the Party as you have ever been."

The morrow had come for everyone, except for the Successor. So it had been laid down that these words would never be heard by their addressee. The extension of the plenum — this delay that had prompted the Guide to say, "All the comrades on the Politburo have expressed themselves, now it's my turn to speak, but since it's so late, I think it's preferable for me to leave my speech until tomorrow morning" — had therefore turned out to be fatal for the Successor.

The adjournment, that isthmus of time between Monday and Tuesday, the furrow that the Successor had been unable to stride over, had tipped him into the abyss. Everybody had been present at his pardon except the man pardoned.

People in the meeting halls began by stages to feel a great sadness. How was it that a man who had put up with anxieties and irritations throughout that unending autumn had been unable to endure one more night of worry? Why had he been in such a hurry?

The Guide's voice droned on in tones no less merciful, and at times it even almost broke into a lament. Members of the audience stole glances at each other: ah, what things the Successor had missed!

But the wave of regret was suddenly crossed by a kind of glacial current. How far could such feelings go? The suspicion that had been nagging at them all morning reasserted itself. There was something very unnatural about all this. The words they were hearing were from the Monday, when the Successor was still alive, but they had not been spoken until the Tuesday, when he was no more than a cadaver. Breaking the rule of the passage of time, the past had been made present. The day before, the day after. It was enough to make them all feel lost.

In the course of the afternoon, people's feelings of bewilderment evaporated. They were seized instead by unusual agitation as they recalled the main lines of the story: the Successor's mistake, the atypical nature of the announcement of his death, the absence of a day of mourning, the rumours about that famous silhouette, the suspicions. Then, as if that had not been enough, now they had to cope with a permutation between Monday and Tuesday. That really took the cake! A cramp in time was, it seemed, something that a capital was least able to tolerate.

5

"Albania continues to live with the unsolved mystery of the Successor" was the more or less standard sentence at the start of reports now finding their way into intelligence agencies around the world.

Given the two long-familiar hypotheses — murder or suicide — supporters of the second alternative still wondered: Why was he killed, and by whom? It was logical to expect that the answer to one of the questions would help to solve the other. To date, however, there was no sign of any answers whatsoever.

Meanwhile, an Icelandic medium, who had taken a second stab at the mystery of the Successor, had finally managed to get somewhere with it. The deep sounds of the dead man's death rattle reached him as through a winter squall. Among those sounds had been heard something about the night of December 13, and also about a woman, or more precisely about two women, either one of whom excluded the other for the good reason that the presence of one of these women made the presence of the other abnormal, and in fact impossible. Between the Successor and these two women there was some sort of debt or arrears, which could equally well be interpreted as a request, a promise, or even a threat. The medium's explanations, written up very oddly, aside from the passages in German and Latin, raised knowing smiles in intelligence agencies. To believe that the enigma of the Successor might be wrapped up in a story of rival women showed a profound misunderstanding of the Communist universe. To the Icelander's great despair, that was pretty much all the response he got from intelligence analysts.

At the same moment, more than a thousand miles away, at the place where the events had occurred, the Guide's speech that had been delivered right after the announcement of the death now plunged the Albanian capital into a frenzy of guess-work. Nonetheless, through the fog of supposition, you could possibly theorise that the case might be reopened, and perhaps that the Successor might even be rehabilitated: there was that autopsy carried out rather late in the day, then there was this new inquiry into the circumstances of the death, alongside rumours that if they had not been officially prompted were probably being actively tolerated (such as the one about the "shadow" slipping into the residence under cover of darkness, or the one about the two men glimpsed by a housekeeper as they accompanied the

Successor down to the basement, or alternatively manhandled his corpse down the steps), and so on and so forth.

If the new investigation was intended to bring back to the fore the supposition of murder, then the Successor would probably end up as a Martyr of the Revolution, the victim of assasination by a group of evil conspirators — an extremely common scenario in Communist countries.

One of the new analysts advanced the idea that it was likely the Successor would wander *ad aeternam* from one hypothesis to another like a damned soul wandering through the circles of Dante's inferno. The last words of the sentence — beginning "like a damned soul" and ending with "Dante's inferno" — were subsequently erased from the report by the writer, who wanted to hold them in reserve for future use, maybe in his memoirs.

THREE

FOND MEMORIES

1

The morning would have been like any other if "they" hadn't turned up so early. But they might as well be here, Suzana thought, as she stuffed her head under the pillow. She had been expecting them for several days. It felt like they had been dragging their feet, that they'd dropped the autopsy and all the rest. So that's fine, she said to herself as she tried once again to get back to sleep. But something unusual about the noise they were making prompted her to get up instead.

Her brother was standing in the half-light in the middle of the hallway, nervously biting his fingernails. Before she had time to ask him, What's going on? he nodded toward the bedroom door. A narrow slit of light shone from underneath, unnervingly, like the last time.

A very distinct but muffled noise could be heard coming from the room.

"They're firing shots in Papa's bedroom," the young man whispered in explanation.

"What?" she exclaimed.

"They're firing a gun. But don't be afraid."

"You're out of your mind!" the young woman replied.

Her brother did not respond. Instead, he stretched his head towards the door, almost losing his balance on his long legs. Suzana realised that his nightshirt must be open, revealing his bare chest; her mind a blank, she tried to do it up, but could not find the buttons.

Then there was another thud, clearly audible in spite of its dull tone. You're all completely insane! Suzana thought. In her sleep-waking mind, the idea that someone was assassinating her father anew, or rather, murdering his corpse, seemed as plausible as it was insane.

She felt that her brother was about to rush toward the door, and she grabbed his hand tightly.

"Wait!"

They stood side by side, almost glued to each other, in total silence, hearing only each other's breathing, until the door opened. Against the light that streamed forth from it they could make out the shape of a man hurrying out. He was holding a revolver, without any doubt the one he had just fired.

The young woman felt she was not in a state to ask the question "So what are you doing here?" or even the words "madness" or "horror". Through the half-open door, on the heels of the man with the gun, came two others, wearing white coats and holding various implements in their hands. Oh no! Suzana groaned to herself. The implements looked as if they had been splashed by blood. Then, to make bad worse, a fourth man emerged, carrying in his outstretched arms a receptacle containing a huge chunk of raw meat.

What a nightmare! Suzana thought as she buried her head on her brother's shoulder. It was probably only one of those bad dreams she'd been having more and more of lately. She dug her nails into her brother's hand, but that didn't help to wake her up at all. "Don't be afraid," he kept saying to comfort her. "They're doing weapons trials." One of the experts had just explained it all to him. "Do you understand?"

Suzana wasn't listening. He put his mouth to her ear, to explain the details that were most painful to understand. "They're conducting tests, to check whether the gunshot could or could not have been heard outside, got it? The trials had to be done by shooting into flesh, in this case a hunk of beef, because a gunshot has a sound like nothing else when it's fired point-blank."

Some part of all that was at last making its way into Suzana's brain.

"Where did you get all these details?" she interrupted. "Are you collaborating with them?"

Now it was the young man's turn to say, "You're out of your mind!"

For days on end, the two of them had shared their suspicions about this or that member of their clan they thought had been involved in the murder.

The young man put an arm around his sister's shoulder, to lead her back to her bedroom. She was grateful to him for not having said, So you aren't satisfied with being the cause of this catastrophe, you also have to get on our nerves with your stupid questions! The bloodied implements that had so scared her a moment ago were there, like all the rest of the setup, for their own good. Thanks to these tests, she and her family might possibly be going back to the life they had known before.

Once she was alone, she passed her right hand over her breast, then her belly, then lower down. The feeling was still very diffuse, but it prompted her to think that she had not made love for five months now. Desire, which she thought she would never feel again, had returned, and it was more insistent than ever.

Five months, she thought. How could that be? She had always thought she could not go more than a week without making love, yet she'd been living like a nun for five months!

The memory of her last stay with Genc, at the villa by the sea, began to unfold in her mind. It had been in mid-September, after the engagement party. It was the end of the season, and the villas all around were closing up one by one. Though it had not been cold, they had made a fire in the hearth. Then they lay down stark naked, something they had recently come to like doing. His desire, and shortly after, her groans, had been unusually intense. Though it was not his habit, he too had moaned a little, sounding like a wounded man.

"Anything wrong?" she asked immediately, still panting for breath. Then with a bitter smile she remarked that right after an orgasm partners' minds always switch back to what they had been worrying about that day.

Genc looked her straight in the eye. "Have you heard anything at all?"

She nodded. Of course she had heard certain rumours that were making the rounds, even inside the *Bllok*. But she'd told herself they were not as important as they might seem. It's a well-known fact that engagements always prompt gossip.

He said nothing.

Suzana gently stroked the fluffy edges of his hair.

"Even if you won't admit it, you felt the effect," he said.

She didn't deny being annoyed, but not for the reason he supposed.

"It's not easy for me to explain it to you . . . It's connected to a kind of obstacle that's been bothering me for a long time . . . Do you understand? . . . I mean . . . I so much wanted this thing to happen . . . more than you can even imagine . . . and now *this* is happening — to me?"

"But what has happened to you?" Genc broke in. "You yourself pointed out that wagging tongues are par for the course in these kinds of circumstances . . ."

"Of course, that's the way things are . . . That doesn't prevent it from being like a barrier, a disenchantment, I don't know how to explain it . . . In something as delicate as love, a mere trifle can sometimes wreck all the joy you feel."

Out of the corner of his eye he studied her wavy auburn hair, as if he was trying to guess what path the thoughts beneath it were taking. That was something she had said, on that unforgettable day when for the first time they had undressed and lain down together in the same bed. With trembling hands she had taken off her summer dress, then her underwear. Her eyes were clouded by desire, and she did not notice his hesitation. She was whispering things she never dreamed she would be able to say while stroking him so brazenly . . . "I love to make love, especially this way, like that . . . you see? . . . you put me in such a state" . . . when she suddenly became aware he was not at ease. "Don't be afraid, I'm not a virgin," she whispered, thinking she had guessed the reason for his holding back. "Haven't been for a long while, you know . . . Come on, my darling," she began again, in a throaty plea, offering herself to him even more provocatively, almost exasperatedly, as if she was under the sway of some blind rage, whereas he only turned his head to the side, as if he had been found out. No, he couldn't do it, he started explaining. It was the first time. It had never happened to him before with anyone else.

She had tried to hang on to the outrage that the words "anyone else" had provoked. Knowing full well she was in the wrong, that she was acting like a spoiled brat, she could not manage to break free of her anger: so, it all went swimmingly with *anyone else*, but what she got was sweet nothing!

"Listen, will you listen to me . . ." He tried to explain in straightforward terms that things were not at all as she thought. Not only was that not the reason, it was the opposite of the truth. His incapacity was the direct result of how much he adored her.

She had meant to interrupt him, to say she'd already heard that old refrain. At school dances, boys in her class were as hot as hell when they brushed up against the other girls, but when they had to partner her on the floor, they went stone cold, as if they were bewitched. Their cheeks turned bright red, to be sure, and their hands were unsteady, but not from temptation, as you might first have thought, but rather from the opposite. From the waist down they became limp. Instead of pressing themselves up to her, they kept a

76

safe distance, but went wild a few minutes later when they were up against other girls.

It was more or less what he was trying to tell her himself. The daughter of a top leader aroused desire as well as respect and fear, but it was the last that always overcame the other feelings. All the more so in his case, because of the additional factor of his own background. She heard disconnected fragments of sentences about Genc's father: a seismologist, studied in Vienna under the monarchy, uncertainty forever hovering over the fate of the family . . .

She had listened to these paltry excuses with an ironical glint in her eye, for what she could hear herself saying inwardly was like a lament: why does it have to happen to me? . . . As her stifled resentment showed no sign of abating, she blurted out harshly a question so sour that she immediately regretted saying it: "Does fear of dictatorship unman you to that extent?"

The young man bit his lip. She had tried to minimise the effect of her words by adding, in a joking tone, "Are we really so terrifying, my father and I? . . ."

The despair that was written on the boy's face seemed irremediable. She had taken his hand, bent to kiss it, placed it on her breast, then between her legs.

Abandoning all modesty made things easier for her. "Don't look away," she said sweetly. "Does it look black and threatening to you? More fearsome, more sombre than the dictatorship of the proletariat? Say something, darling!"

He had not responded. Naked as she was, Suzana got up and walked over to the window. She gazed for a while at the empty beach. The sea was cold and grey. In the far distance you could make out the shape of a woman walking along the water's edge. Had she not known it was her mother, she would not have recognised her. The long shawl draped over her shoulders made her gait look even more eerie. Suzana could feel a grimace distorting her features. She thought of her mother imagining her daughter's orgasm. Poor Mama, if only she knew! she sighed to herself. A month ago, when she had told her mother about the boy she had just met, the older woman had shown Suzana a degree of tolerance for the first time in her life. Suzana had laid her heart bare with all her passion. She told her mother about things they had never spoken of before. In plain words, without shame, she spoke about her physical suffering. Since she had broken off . . . or rather, been forced to break off . . . with her first love,

she had been living in hell. It wasn't just a matter of
emotional suffering, which her mother might have
thought a spoiled girl's luxury, but something else,
which no one dared admit to: it had been physical torture. After two years of regular sexual relations, her
body had suddenly been obliged to cut itself off from
that whole world. She had obeyed her father's injunc-
tion, she had yielded to the argument of force majeure
relating to his career. She had been as meek as a lamb
in respecting his wishes and in renouncing the most
sublime pleasure that this world has to give. But it
could not go on forever. She had at last met a boy she
liked. Both of them took matters seriously, of course,
and intended to get engaged, but she needed to see
more of him to get to know him better. For well-
known reasons, that seemed impossible: because of
the guards, because of the *Bllok* where they lived,
because the *Sigurimi* kept on her tail whenever she
went into town. Only her mother could have the
torture suspended. By helping them see each other,
discreetly, from time to time. For example, at the villa
on the shore, in the off-season . . . To Suzana's great
surprise, her mother did not say no.

Suzana carried on watching the figure on the

beach going back and forth, and for the third time she thought: poor Mama . . .

Then with that special, almost balletlike stride inspired by being naked without embarrassment, Suzana went back to her fiancé. He was all huddled over, gazing at the flames in the hearth with a mindless stare.

She sat herself casually in his lap. "Tell me about the other girls," she whispered with all trace of rancour gone. "You tell me yours first, then I'll tell you mine." His answer was curt: "Don't want to." She stroked his hair and the back of his neck in an attempt to bring him around, but he jerked her hand away: "You're wrong, that's not what's bothering me. Anyway . . ." "Anyway what?" she tried to tease . . . "Anyway, it would have been amazing if things had gone normally. All of you exude such terror . . ." "What!?" Suzana yelled — but Genc hurriedly added, "It's nothing, nothing, forget it . . ." In the deathly silence that suddenly followed, it was he who gently brushed her wavy hair and whispered, "Okay, okay, I'll tell you . . ." She listened distractedly and without really concentrating on a story about a hospital where he'd had to go with a broken leg and where the nurse, who was a bit older than he, got into bed with him; then there was a classmate at university, then another fling during some Youth Movement work experience in the north of the country.

"So you didn't have any problems anytime at all?" she asked after a pause. "You saved that for me, did you?" He shook his head the way people do when they utter a "no" separately, prior to contradicting their interlocutor. Each in turn was in the grip of resentment, as blind as ever. "How can you not realise you are different from the others?" he kept asking her. "You are *other*, you must understand, totally *other*." She didn't know how to take those terms. On the one hand they seemed reassuring, on the other they did not. And when he asked her to tell him about her single love affair, she put such passion into the way she told the tale that he could see how much she was still trying to get back at him. In any other circumstance, she would have talked about it more plainly, but that day, spite prompted her to describe the affair in incandescent terms, without a thought for the pain she might cause her boyfriend. "You described me as 'other', didn't you? Well, *he* was really different, in every sense of the word! He had no respect and no fear. You could have taken him for a silent opponent of the regime. But he probably wasn't anything of the kind. He was simply indifferent. Indifferent, but domineering." She had yielded to him, as people say, on their first date. She was then barely seventeen. After deflowering her, any man, at the sight of the signs proving the fact, would have shown if not fear, at least some concern. But he didn't even comment on it. And she understood at that moment that he was the man she had ardently hoped for. She fell madly in love with him. Maybe he was in love with her? But he uttered words of love only at rare intervals. Each time he penetrated her she thought she perceived in his ardour some secret torment, as if he had been seeking something else in the deep recesses of her body. The mystery and the silence in which he enveloped himself became catching. So it was that one day, when he clumsily let slip that he had already been engaged, she, who on any other occasion would have flown into a rage, demanded an explanation, and burst into tears and recriminations, just bowed her head without a word. Their relationship went on in that way for a long time, until the day the affair was discovered. It coincided with the time when her father was in the process of being officially designated as the Successor. It was very probably the new star that had suddenly begun to shine brightly over her father's career that was responsible for bringing the affair to light. In cut-glass terms, without harping on what her daughter had done, but leaving her no option about future disobedience, her mother had demanded instant separation. "Your father is about to be designated as the next *Prijs*. You have to do this for him. Otherwise we will have no option but to have your lover interned, together with all his close and distant relatives."

Suzana stared at her mother with wild eyes. Intern the man who had made her so happy? "You are out of your mind!" she shouted. "It's you who's lost your head and doesn't want to understand," her mother riposted. And she went on to spill out her heart: "You had the cheek to go with that hooligan, and now you want to defend him!" "He's not a hooligan," Suzana retorted. She almost added that he was the man who had made a woman of her, but she thought better of it as she realised that even if the argument with her mother went on for a thousand years, they would never agree on that.

Forty-eight hours later, her father asked to see her. The wide bay windows of his office seemed to emit a constant vibration, as if they were forever being battered by winds. Suzana felt freezing cold. She was aware that she would not say any of the sentences she had prepared for this interview. What could her father know about her body? How could she tell him about her breasts and her hips aching for caresses, or about her genitals, where pain and sensuality fatally merged and consumed each other? About renouncing lovemaking, when she counted the days, the hours, and the minutes that brought her closer to each encounter? When she still did not understand how, despite the heavenly evanescence that made everything in her fall apart and melt like wax, her body retained its solid shape? He and his comrades had other kinds of pleasures, what with their congresses, their flags, their anthems, and their cemetery of National Martyrs, whereas she only had him . . . his body . . . his inexhaustible body . . .

Her father stared at her with his fair eyes, whose coldness oddly seemed more bearable that day. She felt that the look in her own eyes was of the same kind — alien and distant.

For a long while he said nothing. Then, when he began to speak, she realised right away that it was not only his tone of voice but also his words and his diction that had changed. And it was indeed about a change that he spoke. As from now, her father would no longer be what he had been up to then. What a designated Successor actually was could not be known except by becoming one . . . He would not go on about it, but would only say this to her: people believed he would now be more powerful than ever. That was only half the truth. The other half he would tell her, and her alone: he would henceforth be more powerful and more vulnerable than ever . . . "I hope you understand me, daughter dear."

Suzana listened to him with her head hung low. A wordless flash of light as cold as steel had suddenly made transparent what ought to have taken her days or weeks to grasp. When she felt she could not hold back her tears much longer, she looked up and nodded her assent. Her father looked fuzzy, as seen through a haze, still standing as she turned to leave. At the door she burst into sobs, and as she ran up the stairs to her room she thought she could hear her tears dripping to the floor.

That was how her one and only affair had ended. When she met her lover for the showdown, she had tried to maintain a degree of discretion. She did not mention that he was in danger of relegation, nor did she mention her own quarrel with her mother. All the same, after making love, and still in the thrall of her pleasure, she had not hidden the fact that she was

85

sacrificing herself for the sake of her father's career. He listened to her with furrowed brow, without really grasping what she meant to say. Later on, when she came back to the matter, he must have got the gist in the end. He didn't say a word, but, after a long pause, he muttered something about such sacrifices reminding him of ancient tales that he'd assumed were things of the distant past.

Those were the last words they spoke to each other.

"So that's how it was . . ." Suzana's fiancé kept his eyes fixed on her as she told her story. "Did I make you angry, darling?" she asked as she stroked the back of his head. "There's no reason you should be, that's all ancient history now" . . . No, curiously he didn't seem to have been distressed by the story. As she spoke, something had changed inside him. She could not quite identify which detail of the story had prompted his transformation, but, suddenly, leaning his lips towards her ear, he interrupted her in a whisper and said, "Are you going to show me your dark mystery again, then? . . ."

Glowing with joy she reached out to him with trembling hands. "My love, my love," she murmured when he first touched her between the legs. Her screams turned into a muffled sob before reawakening as a succession of spasms. When the young man withdrew, she kept her eyes half closed. "How beautiful you are!" he whispered to her. Without opening her eyes she replied "It's you who make me so."

Still panting for breath, she covered him in kisses and smothered him in endearments. "Shall we do it again? We'll do it again in the evening, in the afternoon, at dawn, won't we?" "Absolutely," he said, as he fumbled around for a cigarette.

2

Suzana snuggled under the blanket, relaxed her body, and tried to get back to sleep. Never had she felt so exhausted by an act of recollection. Her cheeks were as wet as before. So was her pubic hair.

Outside, dawn was breaking. The whole abomination seemed to be coming to an end. The autopsies, the white-coated judges, the instruments and the measurements would surely have an effect in due course. Poor Papa, honour would befall him late in the day. But at least his soul would rest in peace. As for them, her mother, her brother, and herself, life would go on. Without him, of course, without his dangerous eminence; they would go back into their shells with their heads down, and hope to find warmth to share inside.

That was the advice they got from their aunt Memë, the only person who came to see them in the days of desolation right after the tragedy: stick together and keep each other warm.

She'd turned up before dawn from the remotest part of the south on a train that seemed to have been invented specially for her, wearing a black headscarf bespattered with drops of snow or sleet garnered in unlikely locations.

As surprised as she was anxious, Suzana stared at the unfamiliar old woman, who had been knocking for some while at the door.

"I'm your aunt Memë, I've come to visit," the caller said, raising her voice.

Suzana shouted up from the bottom of the stairs, "Mama, Aunt Memë's come to see us!"

She had thought that her mother would be somehow glad that after their protracted isolation someone had at last come knocking at their door. But her mother's eyes, puffy from insomnia or else from deep sleep, looked the old lady up and down superciliously, as if she didn't recognise her.

"You've forgotten me, but I won't hold it against you. Since God has not yet called me to him, I was just wondering: for what trial has he spared me?"

In outdated language that Suzana only half understood, Aunt Memë rattled off her advice. Most of it began with a negative: "Do not." Do not open the door, whoever calls; do not remember anything, not even your own dreams; do not try to guess whose hand struck down your unhappy father; for although one hand may hide another, behind the other there is always the hand of God. "As for you, my child," she said to Suzana, "stop thinking you're the cause of it all." "Nor should you, my boy," she added, turning toward Suzana's brother, "nor should you think you have to take revenge. But above all," she said to Suzana's mother, you who are a mourning widow, you must not think about it anymore. "What's done cannot be undone, and what's undone is not for mending. Forget so that you may be forgotten."

Suzana's mother kept her eyes on the old lady as she made her speech, staring blankly except for moments when panic welled up in them.

Faint nostalgia for family members relegated to obscure rural outposts came back confusedly to Suzana's mind — relatives who sometimes resurfaced under the guise of remorse, but quickly disappeared again.

Aunt Memë didn't blame them, nor did she let fly with all the resentment she felt. She recited her list of "do not's", and was visibly satisfied not only to see that they had caught the young man's imagination, but that after coffee he took her aside to talk about them further, in private.

"Forget so that you may be forgotten," Suzana muttered to herself, going over her aunt's advice. Easier said than done, even if you restrict it to dreams. Henceforth half of her whole existence, not to say the most substantial part of her life, was made up of memories and dreams.

It was still April, but the inescapable and sparkling month of May, with at its head the first of the month — a day revered like a god — was about to cross the border and make its grand entrance.

Never before could she have dreamt that the hardest day of her life would be invaded by marching crowds, big drums, placards, little red flags and brass bands broadcast over the loudspeakers in the street.

Pictures of her father were more numerous than ever before, waving amid the procession, right behind the portraits of the Guide.

She was on the platform, staring at the unending tide of people in the procession. At times it made her dizzy. A pang of anxiety went through her as she wondered if the man was still expecting her to come to the apartment on Pine Street. Which of her words was he thinking over? If I'm not there by eight-thirty that will mean we will never see each other again. I shall love you all my life. And if I live twice, I will love you both my lives.

From time to time she stole a glance at the central platform where her father stood to the right of the *Prijs*, waving at the crowd, accompanied by the crackling of photographers' flashbulbs. She waited a few minutes, then discreetly looked again, as if to make sure nothing had changed, and she didn't know whether to be glad or saddened that it was all still there, with her father in exactly the same place, at the Guide's side, two paces behind him. Her tired-out brain ran disjointed dreams before her eyes: her father stepping two paces backward, herself pushing through the dignitaries toward him and saying: Father, sir, so you are in the end not the designated Successor? You just said that to deceive me, didn't you? If that's right, then you must release me, Father, sir, so that I can go back to my lover, tear off my clothes, and melt in his arms.

The commemorative banquet was just as awful. The lavish table, the toasts wishing her father ever greater success, and which he pretended not to hear, putting on that distant smile that was meant for no one in particular, plunged her into a state of numbness, where scattered fragments of scenes and sentences mostly unrelated to each other floated around in her drowning mind.

The distinguished assembly at her table made her see it more and more as the altar on which she would be required to lie, to be sacrificed, surrounded by candles. Her eyes sometimes caught her mother's glance. Father, sir, let all this be at least of some use! That's what she believed she was thinking as she watched her father's face, looking like a young bridegroom flabbergasted by his own good fortune. He had disposed of his daughter's fiancé so as to proclaim *himself* the groom at this nightmare banquet.

Quite unexpectedly, it turned windy and rainy in the afternoon of that first of May. Suzana spent the whole of it locked in her bedroom, sobbing.

It was the same bed as the one in which she was

now awakening, without quite managing to figure out to which level of time she was returning.

3

At last she got up. Her eyes were swollen, but this time the thought that had always first come to mind these past few months — what's the point of looking pretty? — didn't even occur to her.

The residence was quiet. It seemed scarcely credible that only a few hours earlier men with guns and instruments had been tramping from one room to another. Her brother had gone out, as he usually did. Her mother was probably out as well. She went up to her father's bedroom door, as she had done so many times before, and tried the handle. It was locked, as it always was.

She went back to her mirror, moved a lock of hair out of the way, examined a spot on her face, then took up her hairbrush. She felt she had forgotten even what it really meant to do her own hair, a practice tied up in so many ways with being beautiful.

Her brother's bedroom door was ajar. She looked in at the table untidily piled high with books. It was here, where no one was allowed to go, that her brother had shut himself up for ages with Aunt Memë.

She had seen them come downstairs afterwards and then wander around the house, in and out the back door to the garden, with him leaning over and with his spidery arms around her, so that her twisted figure all in black looked like his secret torment.

Aunt Memë left in the afternoon, but her shadow and her words stayed on in the house. Suzana's brother made no effort to hide his interest in the dark mysteries of their family's past — for instance, in the curse that people in Tirana would not stop gossiping about. He wanted to know which part of the curse related to the house, and which part to the family, or to the layout of doors and thresholds. As well as the precise spot where the misfortune had arisen.

On that last point brother and sister didn't know what to believe. If a curse really existed, was it to be found in the old part of the residence, or in the new-built section? In other words, on which of the house's two levels did it fall?

As they went on discussing the matter, Suzana could not get the architect's face out of her mind. She was almost certain that the curse emanated from the rebuilt part of the residence. She'd always been told, since earliest childhood, that before being requisitioned by the new government, the house had belonged to the pianist who played the first waltz at the royal wedding. So even if the pianist had had blood on his hands, it would not concern them at all.

Her brother smiled sourly. He wasn't too sure what the elders would say on the question of a house going from one owner to another. Aunt Memë had been evasive on that point too. "I'm not at home in the present," she sighed. "We used to have other customs, like spells and curses; but now there are rituals I can't make head or tail of. People talk about concresses, blinums, and what have you. Ay, ay, ay!"

When Suzana suggested that the new part of the house probably did not yet have any history, seeing that only her engagement party had ever taken place in it when the plaster was barely dry, her brother shook his head in disagreement. He took the view that crimes moved house with people, until they found walls within which they could hide. If the crimes hadn't been committed within these walls, then they had taken place elsewhere. In the highlands, for instance, during the last war. They called it the War of Liberation, but many people said it had been more like a civil war. In other words, a really dirty dogfight.

"Do you think Papa might have committed any crimes?" Suzana asked, almost wailing.

He didn't hear the question, or pretended not to.

What he said next made her hair stand on end: a wedding snuffed out long before would suddenly demand what was due to it if talk of a new engagement woke it from slumber. So many engagements had been broken by the so-called class struggle!

"You're crazy!" she riposted. "Mad and bad."

He replied that he was neither mad nor bad. But when Suzana burst into tears and protested that she could not bear herself and her engagement being highlighted as the cause of all that had happened, he took her in his arms and stroked her hair at length.

"Let me cry a little longer," she begged when her brother urged her to stop weeping.

The greying wisps of their mother's hair that they had seen on the morning of the tragedy, as she screamed at the deceased, so as to be heard throughout the house — "Woe! What have you done to the Party?" — had as it were become stuck in their minds for days on end. She was grieving for the Party's sake,

Suzana's brother whispered in her ear. Not for her own sake. Nor for ours.

Later on, harking back to that scene, it seemed to Suzana that the mystery of their parents' bond with the Party would forever remain inaccessible to her and her brother. It was a bond stronger than the ties of blood, and by the same token stronger than the knot of marriage.

"In the highlands . . . ," she repeated after him. Atrocities must have been committed up there. And that peculiar bond must have been forged there too.

The nature of such a bond was presumably still little understood, because it was too new. Unlike religious allegiances, it was in competition with the ties of clan and family, because it too was a tie of blood — but with a difference. It wasn't based on inner blood, the blood in your veins, identical to the blood of your family going back a thousand years, according to genetics, but on the other kind, on outer blood. That's to say, on the blood of others, blood they had drunkenly spilled in the name of Doctrine.

Whenever their conversation drifted towards topics of this kind Suzana put her hand to her brother's mouth. "Please don't speak of such things, put them out of your mind!" But in spite of herself, she went over it again and again. Inner blood, outer blood . . .

She turned around on hearing the front door creak on its hinges. It was her brother. "Tirana is awash with rumours!" he said, still out of breath. "Apparently, Papa is going to be rehabilitated!"

"Hold on, tell me everything, from the beginning!"

They sat down in the little lounge on the second floor and lit cigarettes. People everywhere were now saying that no autopsy had been carried out earlier not by oversight but intentionally. They were going so far as to mention names of probable culprits. Suspect number one was Adrian Hasobeu.

"What good news!" Suzana said, and jumped up to give her brother a kiss. She realised almost immediately that, as a result of her morning caresses, she must have left her blouse unbuttoned.

He lit another cigarette and puffed at it energetically, as if he was gasping for air. He was staring at a fixed point on the ceiling, his pupils immobile.

"What's wrong?" she inquired gently. "You were going to say something, and now you seem to have fallen into deep thought."

He smiled at her vaguely.

"Nothing wrong . . . I just wanted to say that from now on we should be prepared."

"Prepared for what?"

"Don't you remember Aunt Memë's final piece of advice? — 'Be prepared, know your words.'"

"Know what we will say . . . You mean, about the night of December 13? But we've already told them everything we know!"

"The old woman wasn't referring to the investigators."

"What did she mean, then?"

His breathing became laboured.

"She meant Papa. Know what you are going to say to him when he appears before you. That's what she was talking about."

"Are you trying to scare the living daylights out of me?" Suzana complained.

"There's no reason for you to be afraid. The old woman's mind works the same way as people's did two thousand years ago. For the ancients, encounters with the dead were unavoidable. It didn't matter so much where the encounter took place — it could be in a dream, in the hereafter, or in our own conscience . . ."

"I dreamt of him twice, but wasn't able to speak to him."

"One day you will. You, me, Mama, we all need to know what we will say to him."

He took his time trying to describe, in the least lugubrious terms possible, the wasteland that, in the imagination of the Ancients, separated this world from the shadow world. Where, as on some station platform or in an airport arrivals hall, the dead by the thousands stand around in little groups waiting for their nearest and dearest. Some are overwhelmed with longing to clasp in their arms those from whom they have been separated, but there are others who with sombre and resentful visage display their wounds, waiting for an explanation. As they hold open the gashes in their bodies, so they turn the pages of law books, gospels, proclamations, the *Kanun*, autopsy reports, and ancient hymns.

Suzana lightly touched the back of her brother's hand. "Brother dearest, that's enough of such horrors! Don't we have enough crosses to bear in this world?"

But he shook his head. One day they would appear before their father, and they had to know what they would tell him. "You first of all," he said, turning to Suzana, "you, the most innocent of us all! The purest! Trampled on more than anyone else. If ever he dared . . ."

"No!" she shouted. "I don't want to speak about it anymore. I've forgiven him."

"I'll take you at your word," he replied. "Your encounter with him might turn out to be just a nostalgic embrace. You might even be able to do without words. But things will be different for Mama."

Suzana did not raise her eyes.

"'You, my wife, you who couldn't get a wink of sleep for three whole months, how do you account for having sunk into deep slumber on the very night of December 13?' He's bound to ask that. And I must say I can't imagine what she'll reply. What pills will she claim to have taken? What medical prescription will serve as her defence?"

There was a long pause. But when he resumed in a barely audible undertone, as if afraid to awaken her, and said, "As for me, it will be even harder . . ." Suzana's weary eyes nearly popped out of their sockets.

"Don't be afraid!" the young man commanded. "It's got nothing to do with what you're thinking. It's going to be hard for me for a quite different reason."

He bit his nails as he spoke. Suzana found it difficult to guess what he was getting at. It surely would be hard for him, no doubt about that. There could be nothing more awkward for a son confronted with a father displaying his bloodstained shirt not to promise to reclaim the blood debt, but to declare the opposite: "Stop waving that shirt about. You are my father — I cannot blame you for what you have done, but I have to tell you that I shall not reclaim your blood."

"Dearest heart," she mumbled to herself, "why do you torture yourself with abominations like that?"

Then, looking like death warmed over, he explained, as if he was talking to himself, why even if the opportunity arose he would not avenge his father's spilled blood. As he'd already told her on a previous occasion, his father's blood was different from blood that had been spilled, it flowed in a different direction, belonged to a different group. Just as their mother's breasts were different. His father, his mother, his blood, her milk, were ruled by different laws. In parades, in songs, and everywhere they had lauded "The Light of the Party", they had chanted "The Party is our Mother". Soon people would be clamouring praise for "The Milk of the Party! The Teats of the Party! The Genitals of the Party!" That was actually how it had all begun in the very earliest Communist cells, where activists (male and female) slept (or did not sleep) together not by human custom, but in accordance with the prescriptions of Doctrine.

His tone grew ever more acerbic as he spoke, but Suzana could not find an opportunity to interject and soothe her brother.

That's how the whole business they did not want to recall must have started. After seizing power, and after they had spawned their own offspring, they turned the other way.

He laughed a bitter laugh.

"They brought us into the world, but you have to realise that that gives us only provisional status. When the hour of duty sounds, they won't hesitate to trample us into the ground if the Party requires it. Like they already trampled on you. As they would have trampled on me, if the Doctrine had called for it."

Suzana finally managed to get a word in. "Dearest heart, please, please stop this!"

"Let me finish," he said in a deathly tone. "I'm not just saying all this. In this room, right here, my own father threatened me personally: 'You are my flesh and blood, but you need to know that if you were ever to betray the Party, I would clap you in irons and turn the key with my own hands.' And by the look in his eye I could see he really meant it. Do you understand what I'm telling you? He would have done what Abraham did three thousand years ago, when God asked him to sacrifice his own son."

Suzana held her head in her hands. As she'd become accustomed to nightmares, now she was just waiting for the sound of her brother's voice to come to an end. But he kept on coming back to the new genetics, which encouraged sons to sell their fathers, fathers to sell their sons, wives to sell their husbands . . . Which is why they had understood nothing about what happened while they were sleeping as deeply as if they'd suffered a stroke, on that night of December 13.

Suzana rose at long last and went into the bathroom. She splashed some cold water on her face. Curiously, the dreadful things her brother had been telling her these past days washed off her as easily as her early-morning nightmares.

Once back in her bedroom, she paused in front of the mirror. She looked over her makeup equipment with tears welling in her eyes. The lipstick seemed to have dried in the tube from long disuse. She wetted it slightly before putting some on. It came out in a colour that looked peculiar, almost treacherous. If her brother had still been beside her, God knows what ghoulish comment he would have made about it.

You must try to think about something else, she told herself. As for that shady old hag Aunt Memë, she's welcome back if she brings a good omen, but if not, good riddance!

You must try to think about other things, she reiterated. Maybe ordinary life will come back in the end. Life as under the old genetics, as her brother would say. Maybe all the others would line up in her father's train to take their leave of this world. A whole generation, all the people who had come down from the highlands in a halo of mystery with a blanket over their shoulders, as they'd been told in school, the whole lot of them would vanish into the mist whence they came.

Oh Lord, make them disappear, let life become livable again! Until the time came for the encounter, down there, in that wasteland where they would have been waiting for many a long year.

She conjured up a picture of herself standing in that desolate place, watching a man with a body all tattered and torn coming toward her from the far distance to take her in.

They would embrace, clasping each other clumsily

as her father tried to avoid her lipstick and she tried not to be touched by the blood on his shirt — but what would she find to say to him after so many years apart?

Words rose to her lips but then slipped away again.

She felt as if she was whirling around and around. It was probably spring fever, the feeling produced by an accumulation of happiness that made her bones feel like jelly.

Her legs took her quite naturally toward the bed. Before letting herself doze, she made a last but fairly casual attempt to find the words she might say to her father on the banks of the funereal river. Father, sir, you didn't trust me, and it's through me that misfortune befell you.

A large part of the day was spent in that way, between her bed and her dressing table.

Several times as she went past the telephone she picked up the receiver because she imagined, though she didn't know why, that after being cut off for so long this line would be the first to be reconnected.

Night was falling when she caught sight of her brother through the window; he was marching up and down the garden like a man possessed. As if all the rest had not been enough, the poor boy was still find-ing new suspicions to torment himself with. It seemed to her that since Aunt Memë's visit they were gnaw-ing at him even more painfully.

Aunt Memë . . . she mused, almost in slow motion. If it really *was* she . . .

She ran down the stairs and up to the small gate, where she waited for her brother to be in earshot before sharing her doubts with him. He listened to her patiently, then, instead of saying, "What's all this nonsense?" or "You call me a lunatic, but look at you!" he whispered by way of reply that the same suspicion had occurred to him, but he'd not mentioned it because he didn't want to frighten her.

"But what would be so awful about it, anyway?" Suzana answered, putting on a casual tone that wilted even before she had finished speaking. The worst pos-sibility was that a self-proclaimed aunt had come knocking at their door . . . It's the sort of thing that can happen, especially if . . . especially if . . . they were in the situation they were in.

Sure, such things did happen, her brother mum-bled. But his suspicion was of another kind. Years before — he remembered the occasion clearly — a bereavement telegram had lain in the house without anybody taking any notice of it. Because of the Soviet invasion of Czechoslovakia, Papa and Mama were spending all their time at endless, stressful meetings, so neither of them bothered about the telegram. As he'd only just learned to read at the time, he had a pretty vague memory of what it said. It was the first time he had ever slit open a telegram announcing someone's death. When Aunt Memë had showed up the other day, he'd suddenly had a vision of the thick black line around the edges of that telegram and of the compressed wording that, he thought he recalled, had reported her death.

Suzana's knees nearly gave way. "Are you saying a dead woman came to our door? Are you trying to frighten me to death? Answer me: is that what you want?"

"Sissy!" he retorted. "Do the departed scare you to death? What do you think you are? What do you think all of our kind are? We're the walking dead. Ghosts who scare the daylights out of decent folk. Yes, that's what we are! Ghosts!"

"Oh no," Suzana pleaded, "don't say that. Dearest heart, please don't say such things. Just this morning you were so full of hope, and I was too. What's happened to you?"

He said he was sorry. He hadn't changed. Nor had he had any bad news. It was just his nerves giving way.

He smoothed down her hair and uttered words of comfort, words of hope. All the signs remained as favourable as before. Even the appearance of Aunt Memë wasn't necessarily a bad omen. Whether the old woman was really a *Sigurimi* officer in disguise or a shadow that had come out of a country graveyard, she was altogether preferable to the nothingness that had been their lot up to then, to that deathly hush unbroken by any knock on the door, a door as silent as the stone lid of a burial chamber.

Suzana calmed down and went back inside. In the corridor she thought she heard her mother's bedroom door being slowly pulled closed. She had the impression that her mother had been looking very worried recently whenever she caught sight of Suzana and her brother deep in conversation.

She awoke on the stroke of midnight. She got up to make a complete tour of the house, a recent habit. An ice-pale moon shone through the windowpanes. To her great surprise, the door to the first-floor lounge looked as if it was ajar. She hurried toward it. Yes, it was. Probably the investigators had left it like that in the morning. It was the first time they had forgotten to close that door since December. But maybe it was no accident. Maybe it was the result of the general change in the atmosphere.

Her hand went toward the light switch, but pulled back. There were guards outside who were probably spying on every movement inside the house. Anyway, there was no need to switch on the light. Moonlight streamed into the room, making it look as if it was full of mist. Tears came into her eyes. The room was as unreal as it was in her imagination. Unbearably convincing morsels of the memory of her engagement party sprang up before her eyes. By the marble mantelpiece, her fiancé sipping champagne with two of his comrades. A little farther away, with his back turned, was her father in his dark suit. Then a newcomer, holding a bunch of red flowers, at the head of a merry group. Flashbulbs crackled. Someone saying, "But where is Suzana?" — then, once again, she saw the architect, weeping with emotion. Then everyone going stiff, and voices whispering, "The *Prijs*! The Guide is coming!" Then as soon as he had come into the room, everything went rigid again, but this time it was with the brittleness of glass, sparkling all the more brightly for the complete silence that fell on the party.

"Didn't I tell you he was almost blind?" Suzana jerked her head to the side as if to shake off the secret her brother was telling her.

Despite the efforts he made to hide it, the Guide's blindness was obvious from his every movement. Even his voice seemed affected by his infirmity. "My best wishes! May the happy couple prosper and multiply!" had been said in his deep-throated tone as he looked around for the betrothed. Suzana stood stock-still, unable to decide whether it was easier to bear a clouded gaze than one that was too piercing.

Before he left, the Guide had embraced her father again. They must have been having a heartfelt conversation, as they seemed unable to part from each other; they both seemed to be swaying on their feet together, waving like reeds caught in a gust of wind. When finally they let each other go, Suzana noticed that there were teardrops in the blind man's eyes; but just as she was pondering how all eyes secrete the same kind of tears, her mother's high-pitched voice broke in with a "Would you like a tour of the house?"

Every time Suzana had thought back on it she felt the same malaise about the Guide's slow progress towards the antechamber.

She now followed the same route. In the milky

light of the moon, the lounge looked enchanted. The finest room in the house: that's what all their family and friends who'd been to visit recently had said. Whereas her brother, looking at the room from the doorway on the eve of her engagement party, had answered her question — "Doesn't it look wonderful?" — with, "Sure it does. Maybe more than it should."

Suzana hastened to join the tour group as if she had been prodded. The Guide's overlong black cloak partly muffled the irregular sound of his footsteps. Suzana could hear her mother's harsh voice, sharp as a cleaver, doing the honours: "And here is the antechamber; everyone agrees it is the best room in the house." What's got into you, Mama? Suzana murmured to herself. Her eyes suddenly met the architect's. They were like burning coals, and it seemed astonishing to Suzana that their jet-black hue made them even more incandescent than if they had been flaming red. Alongside the sparkle and the anxiety caused in turn by the hope of flattery and the fear of deprecatory remarks, there was something else in those eyes that moved between both emotions and diluted them.

As always, her mother's thin and steely voice managed, most oddly, to break through the general hubbub. She was explaining how the lights in the lounge were controlled by a special first of its kind switch that was the first of its kind in Albania. "Not that, Mama!" her daughter quaked once more. But the Guide had stopped in front of the switch that the mistress of the house was pointing out to him. The black cloak that up to then had masked his fumbling steps could not now hide his groping hands. He moved closer to the wall, and, in movements characteristic of the poorly sighted, felt for the switch with his hand. Silence had suddenly fallen all around, but when he managed to turn on the light and make it brighter, he laughed out loud. He turned the switch further, until the light was at maximum strength, then laughed again, ha-ha-ha, as if he'd just found a toy that pleased him. Everyone laughed with him, and the game went on until he began to turn the dimmer down. As the brightness dwindled, little by little everything began to freeze, to go lifeless, until all the many lamps in the room went dark.

Each time she thought back on that turning out of the lights, which had amused the company at the time, she felt overcome with anxiety. Sometimes it seemed to her as if that had been the precise moment when the wind had turned.

Suzana felt worn out again and silently went out of the lounge. Her anxiety seemed to be nearing its end. Such great inner turmoil was only a symptom of its imminent lifting. Among other signs, that the lounge and its antechamber, which had been under seal for so long, were now left open confirmed that the end was nigh.

FOUR

THE FALL

1

She was almost aware of being once again in a dream. The doorway was low, its lintel overhung with a peaceful, almost drowsy creeper, and she still could not work out why she was there. She put out her hand toward the iron ring, but she thought she heard herself knocking even before she had grasped it. Well now, she thought, although she did not feel any great surprise. It was fear that overcame her instead.

She took one step forward, but the knocking, far from halting, came louder and louder. The thuds were coming from the other side, sounding now far away, now very close. "Diabolical door!" Suzana yelled out loud, and woke up with a start. It was almost the same dream she had had two weeks ago, except that the knocking was now even louder than in her dream . . .

What's making them knock like that? she wondered, not without a pang of anxiety. They had the keys and could come and go as they pleased any day of the week.

It was obvious that they could come as they pleased, and they often did. Suzana put the pillow down over her head like a thatch roof and figured she would be able to get back to sleep. The knocking had in fact stopped, but now she could hear feet tramping up the stairs. She also thought she could hear her mother's voice. Suzana pulled her head out from under the pillow. Yes, that was her mother's voice. But she wasn't so much talking as screaming.

The young woman leapt out of bed, but before she got to the door it swung open. The screams seemed to be coming less from her mother's mouth than from her tousled, long-faded hair. "Wake up, my daughter, they've come to evict us! Get up, unhappy daughter!"

Though only half dressed, though the blood had drained from her face, Suzana still managed to grasp the main point. They had two hours maximum to leave the house. A lorry was parked outside and was waiting to take them away. Her brother was already racing down the stairs with armfuls of books.

Suzana needed to stay in her bedroom while she tried to get her hands under control. Then she realised it wasn't her hands that were at fault. It was her brain that was jerking them this way and that. First she believed she should take none of the many objects surrounding her, then she thought on the contrary she should take everything.

The lorry had backed up to the residence with its tailgate almost touching the front door. Suzana could not help noticing the licence plate as she went up to it with her first load of winter clothes: *LU-14 17*. That means it's come from Lushnjë, she thought mechanically. Central Albania. The prime area for relegations.

As she went back upstairs, she passed two soldiers carrying furniture down. Her mother was busying herself on the landing on the second floor. Without looking left or right, her brother was running down the stairs a second time. This time he was carrying not just books but also a large package. Maybe his tape recorder. Or else a typewriter.

Suzana puzzled over the half-open drawers where her underwear was kept. With languorous, hesitant gestures, she took out her cotton underwear, then the sanitary towels her mother had brought back from a trip abroad. As she placed them in her bag, she tried to work out how long her supplies would last. Three months? Four months? She couldn't be sure.

The voice of her mother on the landing could be heard piercing the air. She was talking to Suzana's brother. Probably about his books.

The other drawer where her silk things were kept also put Suzana in a quandary. She stretched out her hand, then withdrew it almost in the same movement. Each garment was in a different style and colour, but for her they all fell into one of two categories: those that were connected to *him*, "Number one", and the others, fewer in number, that she associated with Genc.

She picked up a pair of sky blue panties, the ones she had worn her very first time. It was probably on account of this garment that *he* had come out with these unforgettable words: "I like expensive women." She put it back, then picked it up in a bundle with the rest, then in exasperation let go of it. Everything seemed to her to come down to one blinding, unbearable core: for years, in one way or another, what had been required of her was always one and the same thing — to renounce her love. And *they* always won!

She came close to screaming, No! out loud, as her hands hurriedly swept up the whole lot, like a thief.

The door opened behind her back, and she heard her mother saying, "Faster, my girl!"

They always win, she kept on saying to herself as she went down the staircase. She had tried to protect herself, had bleated feeble protests, like a lamb being led to the slaughter, but she had ended up giving in. And now that has to stop! she yelled inwardly. Her sacrifices had been totally in vain. Nobody had even noticed. Except her first man. He who had been destined for the sorry fate that was now hers.

Suzana felt tears streaming down her cheeks. Cold and salty-tasting, like the tears of any woman with hands made dirty by housework, they just kept on flowing. The kind of tears she would no doubt shed henceforth on a towpath or behind a bush as a local farm worker did up his fly.

"Faster!" her mother shouted again as she walked over to the lorry with a portrait. "You'll have plenty of time to cry later on!"

The soldiers weren't accustomed to this kind of work and loaded the furniture clumsily. The tall mirrors sent back oblique reflections every time they were jolted. They had presumably witnessed the eviction of their former owner, and had been waiting their turn for years.

"Careful, soldier!" her mother commanded in an ever more tinny voice. "Wedge some cardboard underneath so it doesn't shift around too much!"

Dimwit! thought Suzana. Her mother was bustling around the lorry, keeping hold of the portrait with both hands. That was when Suzana saw that it was a portrait of the Guide. "Insane!" she muttered under her breath.

Her brother followed behind with a great pile of things. "There's no room left," one of the soldiers said. The lorry driver and the two plainclothesmen supervising the loading looked at their watches from time to time. The uniformed policemen kept their distance. A bunch of onlookers had gathered on the pavement opposite, to watch the free show.

"Come on, time for you to get in," the driver said, pointing to the back of the lorry. "Make a bit of room for them," he said to the soldiers.

Her brother stretched his long legs and climbed in first. Suzana felt her knees buckling. "Give the old lady a hand," someone said. With deathly eyes, Suzana's mother stared at the soldiers in turn, unwilling to let

go of the portrait. Her son jumped down, roughly took
the picture from her, and pulled her up into the vehi-
cle. Suzana bowed her head.

All of a sudden they were enveloped in the regular rumble and throb of the engine, and the two
women, who had been quiet so far, burst into sobs.
The young man stared at them as if he could not recall
who they were.

2

The lorry was still labouring across Albania's central
highlands while the event was already being talked
about in all the cafés of the capital.

The shock that people registered seemed to be of
a very particular kind. It masqueraded as a precursor of
things to come, but clearly it was actually the final jolt
in a whole series of upsets. Briefly astounded, people
went on to rediscover a feeling they had almost forgotten. Initially diffuse, it grew ever more identifiable,
despite the fog surrounding it, and it became apparent
in due course that what had first looked like blank-
ness, weariness and a kind of lethargy was in fact the
expression of relief. In other circumstances, the word

"plot" would have aroused terror, but on this occasion it was on the verge of being treated as good news. As they went around repeating that word, people came to realise how much they had been tired out by its not having been uttered all winter long.

So there really had been a plot, or a conspiracy, to use the other term, and people not involved in it had no reason to be afraid.

No one was unaware of where campaigns that began with the thin end of the wedge ended up. They might start with a few apparently indulgent relegations for liberal ideas in the cultural field, or for foreign influence, or for new artistic trends . . . Then there would be a meeting at the National Theatre. Then a firing squad on some empty lot on the outskirts of Tirana.

Whereas this time there was an open announcement that the issue was a conspiracy. In other words, a putsch planned by the Successor, an attempt to overthrow the Guide. Which presumably meant he had had loyal henchmen and supporters, secret codes, weapons and staging posts. The Successor would not have done himself in for nothing, would he now, seeing how many times he'd mocked at suicide. So the word "plot" was as reassuring as could be. That is, for people who didn't have bees in their bonnets. That's what separated the guilty from the innocent as cleanly as a knife cuts butter. In past times, nobody ever felt certain of anything. You thought you were as white as snow, and then, without even knowing what you had done, you found you had been subjected to foreign influences. Or that you had been contaminated despite yourself by the wind of liberalism. It wasn't by chance they called them winds of ill fortune — you could get caught out by a diabolical draught anywhere you stood. But this time you couldn't get picked on and blamed, for instance, for making love to your wife incorrectly — in a decadent manner, as they used to say. But could you call that a plot against the state? Come off it, you know what you can do with that kind of nonsense. Decadent behaviour was rightly so called; it wasn't very savoury, to be sure; it was extremely unhealthy for all and certainly unworthy of a Communist, not to mention an official, but you had to face facts: no way could things like that constitute a plot!

The latest news that reached the city's ears at nightfall only made the day's rumours more plausible. In late afternoon, the Successor's tomb had been demolished and his mortal remains bundled up with the planks from his coffin and the soil around it, put in a plastic bag, and removed to an unknown location.

To judge by the way these facts were reported, something seemed to have affected people's linguistic abilities . . . Some kind of petrifaction of language had condensed their stories, and this in turn curiously served to make them more precise. The soil-stained tarpaulin that had been used to carry off the Successor's remains probably revived memories of snatches of ancient epics, parts of which had been dropped from school textbooks as a result of campaigns to eradicate medieval mysticism from the national curriculum.

When, two days later, the Communists assembled once again in fourteen of the city's halls to listen to a speech by the Guide, the last winter winds sweeping down from the hills seemed to bring with them some ill-remembered scenes from the past . . . *In the Yellow Valleys, the fourteen lords of Jutbine foregathered within the walls of their fourteen towers . . .*

The astonishment that had arisen on the previous occasion was provoked once again by the wording on the invitations. The same tape recorder was to be seen on the same small table with its vase of flowers. The Guide's voice was weary and almost off-hand, which spread a sense of menace more effectively than ranting would have. He now hardly bothered to hide the imminence of his own demise; time was too short to waste it on unnecessary words.

So what had happened had been a conspiracy. The most heinous in the whole history of Albania. The most terrifying. Pressured by foreign sponsors, the Successor, the instigator of said conspiracy, had been cornered into making a desperate move — to sacrifice his own daughter. That was the only way he could signal that he was intent on dropping the class struggle and initiating a change of line. He had thrown his own daughter into the maw of the class enemy so as to make his own preference clear to all.

Fear glazed the eyes of everyone listening to the Guide's explanation. The country's history was full of examples of clans who had sacrificed their daughters for the sake of the nation. The celebrated Nora of Kelmend had gone to the tent of the Turkish commander-in-chief not to give herself to him, but to slay him. Whereas he, the Successor, had pushed his daughter into the enemy's clutches for the opposite reason.

Had the wedding taken place, it would have sounded the death knell of Albania.

Silence fell after these final words. The continued humming of the tape recorder made it seem even deeper, so much so that people began to think that they would soon be able to hear the thoughts that were buzzing around in each other's heads. They stayed riveted to their chairs until someone walked quickly and stiffly onto the platform and switched the machine off.

3

The fourteen halls of Tirana were full again a week later. Although the same number of invitations had been sent out as on the previous occasion, the halls seemed particularly crowded this time. The impression that shadows had slipped in between the seats was presumably due to what was coming out of the tape recorder. It was broadcasting the answers given to the interrogators by the Successor's wife, son and daughter. The most serious accusation was made by the wife. Unlike his mother, the son insisted he had not been aware of his father's goings-on, save for a letter he had posted at his father's request during a trip to Rome, which had aroused his curiosity at the time and which, moreover, still puzzled him. As for the daughter, she spoke only about her broken engagement. Her speech, which was confused and broken up by bursts of sobbing, made it sound as though she was not talking about one engagement, but about two, both of which had been shattered for reasons connected to her father's career.

The judge interrupted her in an attempt to get some clarity about the earlier affair, but his question actually made things even murkier. No, her father had not encouraged her, quite the contrary, he had been against her first love insofar as it might be disadvantageous to his career, though from a different angle.

"Our information is that this man, your first sweetheart, was from a Communist family and worked as a journalist at National Television. Is that correct?" "Yes," the young woman concurred. "In other words," the judge went on, "your boyfriend had socialist credentials, and that was enough to make your father stop him ever darkening his doorway."

Suzana's breathing grew faster, distorting her words now and then. The judge reiterated his question, saying that as far as he could see her father had in mind to reserve his daughter's hand for a damaging political marriage, but all she could reply, between two sobs, was: "I don't know!"

The rest of the girl's story — of her tearful pleading that failed to soften her father's heart — could just as well have been about her first love cut brutally short, as about her later engagement, which had been speeded up with a sinister end in view — as was only now becoming clear.

What a cynic that man was! the Party veterans muttered as they left the hall. He offered up his daughter like a lamb — so imagine where he could have led Albania! The country had been really very fortunate in escaping a Successor of that ilk.

As they chatted along these lines, some of the oldest stalwarts nursed private hopes that the Guide would in the end pick a Successor worthy of the name. Many others weren't at all sure that a man deserving to stand that close to the Guide could ever be found. The best that might be done would be to appoint an acting Successor, so to speak, a kind of ante-Successor, if such a title could legitimately be used.

In that case, someone piped up, it was no secret that the only plausible candidate for the post was Adrian Hasobeu. The others nodded. That was obvious. Hadn't he long been thought of as a silent opponent of the Successor? He'd even been suspected of . . .

As they got nearer home, their expressions softened, and when their families set eyes on them they breathed a sigh of relief. Meanwhile, the cleaners who were clearing up the meeting halls, opening doors and windows to let in some air, were surprised by the odd smell that filled the place. It was different from the odour of feet, sheep-wax, and sour milk they had encountered after the assembly of top-ranking herders. It was another smell, one that had been getting more common recently. It was the smell bodies make when they are afraid.

4

Adrian Hasobeu was aware that his name was now on everybody's lips. But whereas rumours of that kind would have kept him awake all night long in days gone by, they now produced quite the opposite effect.

Everything had changed in a flash when the Guide, after tergiversating unendingly throughout the spring, which had been a dark season for Adrian Hasobeu, had reached his decision and denounced the Successor for treason.

Never before in his whole existence had he felt such relief. The slackening of the tension in his limbs and of all that coursed through his lungs, his blood vessels, and his brow made him realise that a part of his being that he had believed dead, but which had in fact only been sleeping, was coming back to life, as if it was slowly emerging from a static bank of fog.

Several members of his clan had gathered under his roof. Near-silence reigned over their solemn presence. They said nothing, but gazed with shared affection at his drawn features. The eldest of his uncles was the only one to put his arms around him, before breaking down in tears.

After lunch, when he told them, "I'm going to take a short rest," the same caring glances fell upon him, alongside muttered have-a-good-nap-have-a-good-rest-sweet-sister-souls.

From his bedroom he lent an ear to the murmurs that his absence had probably revived. It lulled him to a sleep more delicious than any he had known before.

When he woke up, he knew at once that they were still in the house. They were probably even more transported by joy than he was, just as in March, when the house had been almost entirely empty, they had probably been even more distraught than he had been. He didn't feel the slightest resentment for their having abandoned him at that time. He had even strongly advised them to act that way. "It would be better if you didn't show your faces here until things have been cleaned up."

The clarification took its time. Complications arose from the first morning after the Successor's death. His wife had been the first to grill him: "What do you say to the rumours people are spreading about you?"

He didn't answer. A long silence followed, then his wife returned to the attack: even supposing he had really been over there . . . at *his* house . . . around midnight . . . why should it have been divulged? Who had spotted him? In short, why had the gossip not been stopped?

He raised his eyes, with a bitter smile on his lips, but his wife didn't let him get a word in edgeways. "I know what you're going to say — that you can't put a stop to gossip. But you know as well as I do that you can!"

Indeed he knew. Despite that, this first phase, oddly enough, left him cold. At the end of the day, he had got the better of his perfidious rival. Even the suspicion that he had liquidated the Successor somewhat ahead of time served to show only that he'd been excessively eager. It was a well-known fact that, in this kind of case, overeagerness earned not only a reprimand, but also a degree of respect. The mere existence of the suspicion had suddenly enhanced his stature in the eyes of others. Because of it, his promotion to a higher position now seemed only a matter of course. The rumour that he might even be picked to fill the Successor's shoes sprang from the same kind of reasoning.

Things only started to turn the wrong way in March, with news of the autopsy. The scalpels and tongs used to section the Successor's cadaver would have caused him less agony than the fragmentary speculations he heard from all quarters. The autopsy wouldn't have been ordered if there hadn't been doubts. Its results could turn things upside down. The Successor's sudden return in the shape of a martyr could easily cast his rival into the abyss.

The same questions preyed on Adrian Hasobeu's mind from the moment he got up to his going to bed: Why was no one taking up his defence? Why was the Guide not giving him any support?

The latter's eyes appeared to recognise him no longer. It was apparently the last benefit that the onset of total blindness could give him. But as he went over in his mind his last meeting with the Guide,

Adrian Hasobeu still could not see what mistake he had made.

. . . The Politburo meeting seemed to go on forever, on that late afternoon of December 13. The Successor was answering questions with ever sparser sentences. Sometimes he left a pause, as if waiting for the end of some inaudible translation. His eyes remained fixed on the typescript of his self-criticism, on which every now and again he pencilled annotations.

All of a sudden, the Guide took his fob watch out of the pocket of his black jacket. He kept looking at it as the secretary sitting next to him whispered something in his ear, presumably what time the watch said.

The room froze and waited.

"I think it's getting late," the Guide had declared. His eyes were trained on the place where the Successor was sitting. "I propose that we put your self-criticism off until tomorrow . . ."

In the ever deeper silence, most of those present who had attended a similar meeting years before probably recalled the very same sentence being said at more or less the same time of day: "It is getting late; I suggest we leave your self-criticism, Comrade Zhbira, until the morning." Not a muscle twitched on Kano Zhbira's livid face, as if the death mask that would be placed over it the next day, after his suicide, had already begun to turn it into rock.

"Well, then," the Guide resumed, still gazing towards where he thought the Successor was seated. His voice was weary, almost gentle, after such a long day. "As for you, try to get a proper night's sleep, so as to be in good shape for your speech tomorrow. And the rest of you too."

The pallor that had not left the Successor's face was the same, still recognisable colour. Adrian Hasobeu felt his body relax, as if the Guide's wishes for a good night's rest affected him first and foremost. The vague impression that it would once again be at night . . . a transitional night . . . yes, like the last time . . . on a calendrical quirk that only the blind man could control and which cropped up each time the latter invoked the passage of time . . . that idea made him go weak in the knees in anticipation.

He went home in the same half-dead state. He was just getting into bed when he was called to the telephone. The Guide was waiting for him in his office. The old man's eyes were cloudy and his diction even more so. "I have something like a bad intuition about what might happen tonight," he had told him. That's why he had called him in. "You're the only person I trust." What he was asking Hasobeu to do was not very clear. The more he tried to concentrate, the hazier it got. He was supposed to go over to the other man's place. Try to find out what was going on there . . . "Only you can do it."

No help shone from the Guide's dark brown pupils. Only the inscrutable opacity of blind eyes. Twice he thought the Guide was going to give him something, perhaps the keys to that underground passageway, if it really existed. But nothing of the sort occurred. No keys, and no further explanation. He just kept on repeating, "You're the only person I trust." He regurgitated his other assertions as well: he had to go over there on foot, around midnight; when the guards recognised him, he shouldn't worry, he was a minister, it was okay for him to inspect the duty squad in the thick of night . . . not to mention the other . . . then he was to return . . . he, the Guide, would be waiting up for him, eagerly . . .

Adrian Hasobeu did not once dare to interrupt him, and obeyed his instruction: "Now, go." He went. He waited at home for midnight to come, then went out again, alone, on foot, by a side door, wearing his black oilskin cape. The night was dark and wet, cut asunder by lightning at irregular intervals. It was a special night, a night of transition, and he stepped through it as through a nightmare.

From afar he made out the Successor's bedroom. It was the only one on that side of the house that was lit. When he pushed back his cape, the guards recognised him. He paced up and down around the house like a man in a fever, peering at each of the doors as if he still hoped that one of them would suddenly open . . .

A few minutes later, Hasobeu was back in the Guide's office. The *Prijs* had indeed waited up. He even made to move toward Hasobeu.

"Did you do it?" he asked, with unmasked impatience.

Adrian Hasobeu nodded.

Himself stared at Hasobeu's hands as if trying to make out spots of blood on his skin. His gaze was so powerful that it made the minister want to hide his hands behind his back.

All the doors were bolted on the inside.

He wasn't absolutely certain he had said exactly that. *Himself* said, "Now I can sleep peacefully."

Outside, on the path, it was raining harder than ever. Adrian Hasobeu thought he was on his way home, but his feet took him in another direction. When he glimpsed the Successor's bedroom from afar once more, he understood. That's when he took the revolver from the inside pocket in his oilskin and fitted the silencer onto the barrel.

Early next morning, the four telephones in the house rang incessantly. When he arrived at the Successor's residence, he found the state prosecutor had arrived first. His eyes crossed the puffy, insomniac, and desolate gaze of the bereaved wife, and he almost choked on the question: "Who moved the body? I meant to say, has the body been moved?"

He had put such effort into imagining every detail that the sight of the corpse gone cold now seemed quite familiar to him.

At the Politburo meeting, which began an hour later, he sought but failed to catch the Guide's eye. What did *Himself* actually believe? The question nagged at him unrelentingly all that morning, and came back to haunt him even more later on, during that unending week of the autopsy. His last conversation with the leader, the one he'd had with him around midnight on December 13, appeared henceforth like a hallucination. It seemed to have either no sense at all, or far too much. It must have been then that the thread broke. From the moment when, after leaving the Guide, his steps took him back to the

Successor's residence, he had the palpable feeling that something needed to be put right. And that was probably where things had become all tangled up.

Perhaps, like half the population of Tirana, the Guide took him for the killer. Or did he suspect that his minister had intended to commit murder, but hadn't managed to do so, seeing as someone else got his bullet in first? Or that the Successor had beaten both his assassins to the wire by pulling the trigger on himself?

What would he not have given to know even just half the surmises in the mind of *Himself*! Now and again, those surmises would disperse almost instantaneously, like a flock of crows taking fright and leaving a solitary bird in the empty lot they had just abandoned. Shouldn't that crow be put down too, because of everything it was now the only bird to know? That was Adrian Hasobeu's initial hypothesis, elemental in its simplicity, but which he did not find too hard to put aside precisely because it was so simple. It was too ordinary, too well-known to remain part of the Guide's set of mental tools.

No! he said to bolster himself, despite his weariness, and not quite knowing to whom he was really talking. Maybe the Guide did suspect him of having committed murder, especially if he had been told of Hasobeu's second visit to the Successor's house. Or maybe, short of suspecting him of murder, he thought Hasobeu had prompted the suicide . . . that he had gone there to try to corner the man . . . or that he hadn't gone over there at all. The threads had begun to unravel, but Hasobeu himself could no longer clearly see what was true and what was false in such a complicated imbroglio.

On several occasions, he came close to writing a letter to the man *Himself*. He was prepared to assume responsibility for all possible and imaginable crimes — murder, incitement to self-destruction, etcetera — if that could be of use to the Cause. The first lines of his letters provided him with a sense of relief, but then he was overcome with a sense of defeat. He realised with alarm that he had not known how to interpret *his* signs. In fact, the Guide had never been very forthcoming, as, for instance, in the Kano Zhbira affair: each time the body was exhumed, the current winners were cut down, until the next unburying brought down their successors too.

The wall of inscrutability had become even thicker these past few years. His increasingly poor eyesight seemed to give him perceptions that no one else could fathom. Such impenetrable fog that nobody knew what to believe.

Despite knowing all this, in his fit of gloom Adrian Hasobeu felt like shouting out loud: why was it me that *he* had to send over there on the night of December 13? To set me up as a murderer, if a murderer should be needed? At times, he thought there could be no other way of accounting for it. The Successor's death had worn two masks, but one of them would have to be chosen in the end. "If you didn't do it," his wife told him, "there's no reason why you should bear the brunt." He left a long pause, but when his wife repeated her question once again, he replied: neither she nor anyone else would ever understand the first thing about it all.

Something he had recently discovered lay at the root of the incomprehensibility he was referring to. Suspicions were by far the most cherished attributes of the mind of a guide. They formed as it were a pack of hounds, to play with and relax at lonely times. But if anyone dare get too close, beware!

His wife bowed her head while he, feeling almost a sense of relief, tried to explain. It was because the Guide, as far as he could grasp, expected no explanation to be forthcoming that he, Adrian Hasobeu, had refrained from offering any. What he had meant to say by remaining silent was to indicate that he was prepared to accept his fate, or, in other words, that his fate would be whatever the Guide so desired. If you need to brand me as a criminal, then so be it, my Lord! Or whatever else. The choice is yours.

The rumblings of his tribe reached his ears from the main room, and brought him even greater comfort. Above the low hum he could make out little noises as of snaps or muffled clicks, which, oddly enough, far from irritating him, aroused faint nostalgia.

When he got up and opened the door to the main room, he immediately understood why. In the kitchen, on the other side of the hall, his three sisters, together with the servants, were rolling puff pastry. "You look surprised, cousin," one of the visitors said to him. "Could you have forgotten that the day after tomorrow is your birthday?"

One of his sisters, with flour up to her elbows, greeted him with a kiss. "Did you have a good rest, dear heart? We're in the middle of making a baklava like you've never tasted before."

Still in the haze of sleep, he looked on at the layers of pristine pastry piled as high as he remembered on days before weddings in the big house back in the village. He had completely forgotten the date of his birthday, like so much else in the course of that sinister winter.

He asked for a glass of water, then turned back to gaze greedily at those layers of pastry, as if he could never have his fill of the sight of them.

5

Adrian Hasobeu's birthday ought to have marked the very summit of his career, but a few hours of the day were all that was needed to finish him off.

A first, almost imperceptible eddy, faint as a fluttering of wings, arose at about eleven o'clock. Almost the entire government and the majority of the Politburo were in attendance. The *Prijs* was expected any minute. He usually came to this sort of event at about this time. Symptoms included a kind of withdrawal of people to the corners of the room, flagging conversations, and eyes that returned almost in spite of themselves to keep watch on the main door. Even the glasses and bottles seemed to be holding their sparkle back. Adrian Hasobeu was making a superhuman effort not to watch the clock. But the time was plain to see wherever you looked. For the expression on all his guests' faces resembled nothing in the world so much as the round dials of a clock!

Are you all so worried on my behalf? he thought with a touch of bitterness. But he saw immediately that he was being unfair to them. They were all his people, and he would bring them down with him when he fell.

By noon the partygoers' whispering had become incomprehensible and their meaning could only be guessed at.

Though he had already been petrified, so to speak, he still managed to summon up the thought that there was still time for a letter or a telegram to come. There was no written rule that said the Guide always had to attend in person. He couldn't remember when, but it had happened before, he was sure of that, all the more so in view of the ever-declining state of *His* health.

When they took their places at table for the meal, there was an unexpected excitement in the air. The appropriate toasts were proposed, and he managed to keep up appearances. It was only during the last course, when he tried to enjoy the baklava, that the food stuck in his throat. His sister's words came back to his mind, in disorder: a baklava such as . . . a baklava like . . . He tried to put the thought out of his mind but did not succeed. Of such a baklava he had indeed never before partaken, nor had any of his relatives.

After coffee, the guests hung around. He was eager to see the house empty and almost wanted to yell out loud: what are you waiting for, can't you see you're not wanted here anymore?

An unhealthy knot made of strands of blind rancour and of unreleased imprecations like: are you standing around so as to get a better view of my fall? combined with the superstitious idea that maybe *he* was waiting for the floor to be cleared before making his entry, was bringing his mind to a complete standstill.

Dumdfoundedness followed his bout of exasperation. In his prostration, he suddenly saw the naked and implacable notion rise up before him that not only would the Guide not come, but that there would be no letter and no greetings telegram either. Nor would he even call on the telephone.

The sum of it was harsh enough, but an hour

later, when the first shades of dusk spread across the garden, the Guide's absence no longer seemed at all surprising. On the contrary, what now seemed crazy was to nurse the slightest hope that *Himself* would turn up. And it was not just the Guide's presence, but the idea of a birthday card, a greetings telegram, or even a phone call now looked like the idle dreams of a schoolkid. He realised that very soon the downward slide of his despair would be so steep as to make him amazed they hadn't already come to take him away.

After a short interval, the guests had begun to return in numbers. As before, bringing cakes and wine as well as bouquets. The maddest procession you could think of. Weren't they aware there was nothing more that could be done? Except maybe to bring flowers, as they alone could be used at funerals as well as birthdays.

What was even more unbearable than their being here were the birthday wishes. On two occasions he couldn't even understand what they were saying and blurted out, "What was that?" "May you rise ever upward!" they intoned by way of reply.

Try to look your best, his wife whispered in his ear as she pretended to come up to draw the curtains.

He turned to look at the French windows that opened onto the garden. Light was fading fast. It was years since *Himself* had been out so late in the day.

He encountered his wife in the hall once again. She said, "Listen, I never managed to understand why you went back . . . the second time . . . to that place."

He looked her in the eye, at length. So, though she was putting on a good front, she too was thinking only of that.

"Why did I go back?" he answered in a ghostly voice. "You won't believe me, but I tell you I have no idea."

His wife, completely distraught, shook her head. "Haven't you had enough of keeping all these secrets? You've spent your whole life with them!"

He too shook his head, to contradict her. "I have no secrets from you, my wife."

He began softly, almost inaudibly, then suddenly his voice broke into a raging and inhuman bawl: "You really want to know what I did that night? I did *nothing*! Got that? The doors were bolted from the inside."

"Get hold of yourself," she urged.

He was gasping for breath.

"All the same, you must have been expecting

something when you were standing outside the residence," she went on, in a calmer voice.

"I don't know what I was expecting. Of course, I was expecting something . . . Maybe a signal from inside. Or something like that . . . Perhaps it was supposed to be that way . . . Perhaps I had to wait for a sign . . . Maybe I was mistaken . . ."

"A sign *from whom?*"

Nothing was that simple . . . From someone who had been prevented from giving it . . . At least, that was my impression . . . But at no point was there any sign at all . . .

"But that's dreadful!" his wife moaned. "Waiting for a sign you know nothing about . . . not knowing the why or the wherefore . . ."

"That's where I made the wrong move. I failed to pick up the right wavelength . . . What he said to me that night was so unclear. And what he told me later, when I got back to his office, was even murkier. As if he had already gone to sleep . . ."

"That's the worst of our misfortune," his wife blurted out. "Even when he's asleep he treats you like a plaything. But you and your kind, you don't even see it! Wide awake and as blind as bats!"

147

He would have liked to tell her that she had probably hit upon his real secret: how to keep people on a string while fast asleep.

"Go circulate and talk to the guests," she said. "We've been alone too long."

"Are they still there? For God's sake get rid of them for me! Tell them the party's over. Say anything you like as long as it gets them out, and the doors closed!"

6

Six hundred feet away, in the large room he had been using as an office for a while, the Guide, facing the wide bay window, was listening to a secretary reporting on what could be seen going on in the garden that overlooked the rear of the presidential residence.

The last glimmer of daylight made the few trees that had been planted here and there seem to be moving off into the distance. Soon darkness would spread all over, and the dead leaves falling from the trees would no longer be seen at all.

He asked the secretary if the sky was overcast, then he wanted to know if the junket at the Hasobeus' house was still in full swing.

The secretary satisfied both requests: some clouds, and the party had just come to an end.

He must have figured it out, he thought. Now he'll need at least a week to recover.

His stone-cold hatred, reviving after a brief pause, was utterly unbearable.

I gave you almost a year, he addressed his minister in his mind. His mouth filled with bile. That man should never have been granted such a long reprieve.

An old ditty from his hometown came back to mind:

> Those yarns you told
> Were lies too bold;
> Then for this fall
> You promised me all . . .

Hasobeu had disappointed him. Even leaves, mere leaves on a tree, knew when it was time to fall — but that man pretended not to. He now had an interminable week to make amends for his mistake.

Don't force me to bring on the black beast! he thought.

Not wanting to let himself sink into a bad mood before dinner, he tried to think of something else.

"It looks like it's dark outside now," he remarked to his secretary.

"Yes, it's completely dark," the secretary replied. "They've switched on the garden lamps."

FIVE

THE GUIDE

1

The week felt as if it would never end. Friday, when the Central Committee's plenum would meet, was still far off. He spent the whole of Tuesday morning listening to ambassadors' reports and to a summary of the underground news from Tirana. A seventeen-year-old girl in the adjacent quarter had taken her own life. Rumours about Hasobeu's fall were still infrequent. Only one of the wire services mentioned it, and it got the man's name wrong anyway, making it unrecognisable. The girl had killed herself for sentimental reasons. A young swank, who repaired bicycles on the square where she lived, had dropped her. "Haseberg . . ." he muttered, mulling over his minister's mangled name. "Now you're defying me under a Teutonic name!"

While virtual silence reigned on the Hasobeu situation, all the old surmises about the death of the Successor resurfaced, presumably by reaction. Probably an attempt at destabilising the entire Balkan Peninsula. Expansion of the Atlantic alliance to this part of Europe. Oil. Suicide or assassination? The real reason. Who pulled the trigger . . .

"Always the same old stories," he muttered under his breath.

The secretary waited for the Guide's mumbling to cease before going on. The underground passageway. What might have happened in it on the night of December 13.

That last phrase made him sneer. "That's a laugh!" Then he asked the secretary to read it out again. According to the informant, people were saying that the last meeting between the Guide and the Successor took place in the tunnel at midnight. The latter had reached for his gun but the Guide's bodyguard had been quicker on the draw.

The secretary waited for *Himself*'s guffaws to die down before going on. The Successor was supposed to have got himself shot in the basement, so that what had been said about the lifeless body of the victim being brought up the stairs like a tailor's dummy by two men could be incorporated into the story.

"Wait!" the Guide said. "Read that to me once more . . ."

The secretary read it again, this time more slowly, but when he had finished, *Himself* asked to hear it one more time. As he listened, he repeated the sentences under his breath. What had been said . . . in other words, what had been foretold.

"It's like in the holy books," he mumbled dreamily. "In the Bible, unless I'm mistaken, some events are laid out like that."

The secretary looked at his master with veneration, as he did every time the Guide made a reference to what he had read. He put his nose back into the stack of papers, but *Himself* interrupted: "Wait, not so fast!"

At first the secretary did not grasp what the Guide was asking of him. He had been dealing with an abstruse report in which the analyst, after mentioning the mysterious death in Tirana, tried to unravel the functioning of the brain of a dictator.

Placidly, the secretary went back to the report. He'd been in this job for forty years, and in the course of time he had lost more or less everything, including his sense of fear.

The text he finally retrieved was quite brief. According to its author, the brain of a tyrant often worked according to what might be called the "architecture of terror". Terror was constructed backwards, like dreams, which is to say, starting from the end. Then, in a flash, sometimes in a mere second or even less, the entire missing part was suddenly filled in. To make his meaning clearer, the analyst proposed the image of a building constructed out of its own ruins. All the rest — the walls, partitions, roof, chimney and even the furniture — would suddenly be added, then knocked away. That was the process of the Master's mind when passing sentence. First plan the victim's death, and the rest would be fitted in afterwards.

That's what you have done, he thought.

His breathing accelerated from spite. Yes, they had been doing these things themselves since biblical times, and now they were claiming he had invented them!

He became aware of his wife's footsteps behind him.

"There's a letter from Hasobeu," she said as she leaned over his shoulder.

"Really? Let's have a look at the brain functions of . . . von Haseberg!"

The missive struck him as both interminable and cunning. Hasobeu complained of being cold-shouldered even though everything had now been brought out into the open. As long as it had been thought that the Successor might have been a martyr, assassinated by some other hand, suspicions about him, Hasobeu, had been understandable. But now that it had been admitted that the Successor had been a traitor and had killed himself, why was he, Hasobeu, still under a cloud of suspicion?

"You wily hypocrite!" Anger rose inside him. "You think you can pull the wool over *my* eyes, do you?"

His breathing quickened again. Hasobeu was playing innocent in order to get out of the hole he had dug with his own hands. He was pretending things were disarmingly simple: you say the Successor was a murdered martyr? Then you're right to suspect me. But now you say the Successor was a traitor and a suicide. So what can you possibly hold against me, Hasobeu?

"Take this down!" he instructed his secretary. "Hasobeu is conveniently forgetting a third hypothesis, which may well be the right one. Whether the man was a martyr or a traitor, whether he was murdered or killed himself, one thing is clear — Hasobeu was involved. He spent the night prowling around the Successor's residence. Did he or did he not plan to kill him? Did he mean to corner him into taking his own life, which was already a waste of time? Did he or did he not let the murderers into the house? The answers to these questions make not one bit of difference. What we have is typical of conspiracies. As soon as they sniff danger in the wind, the plotters hasten to get rid of the mastermind. Everybody knows that.

"It's been known for all eternity," he mumbled. "Same as the epilogue."

"Take this down," he said to the secretary again. "In my name, you're going to send him a note that you'll sign for me. Invite him to the Central Committee plenum the day after tomorrow, so he can lay out everything he knows. So he can bare his heart!"

He could already hear the deathly hush that would fall upon the meeting when he turned to Hasobeu and called on him to speak. Bare your heart, Hasobeu! We'll soon see who's scared by all the secrets you're going to spill!

Knowing the secrets of everybody around you was indisputably a blessing, but not knowing them was close to being sublime. He'd only recently come to understand that, and it left him in a state of great calm. His blindness had no doubt helped him toward such serenity.

He didn't know, and never had known, what had really happened at the Successor's residence on that night of December 13. And since even he didn't know, it could take a thousand years for anyone else to find out.

Like beasts of another species, they were all circling around him now, trying to explain with miserable whimpers, with all kinds of signals and glances, what in their view had taken place. But they could bark until their lungs were sore; what they had to tell him was necessarily incomplete and incoherent. All they knew of the matter had been seen as through the eyes of an insect, in parts and fragments.

Apart from the deceased, two other individuals seem to have been implicated. But no one would ever know exactly how they had become tangled up in the murky business, where they had crossed paths, when they had put each other off, how they had black-mailed each other until the whole thing fell under the shroud of silence. Only one of them, Hasobeu, had spoken up, half screaming and half moaning: the doors had been bolted on the inside.

He was minister of the interior and seemed not to know that in all great murder cases doors are always bolted on the inside!

He thought he heard the wind rising, and asked what was going on in the garden. If his memory was to be trusted, ancient tragedies dealt exclusively with that: how to expunge the crime, how to detach it from the clan. He didn't recall ever coming across a mention of the opposite problem — how to get a crime to stick.

It was probably the noise of the storks leaving their nests, his secretary told him. The rustling was loud enough to make that the most likely cause.

He heard his wife coming up behind him again, which made him hold back what he was about to say.

"Are you bringing me another letter?" he asked merrily, without turning around.

"Indeed I am," she replied.

Before muttering, unbelievable! he felt the envelope with the tips of his fingers. It had been sent by the Successor's widow.

All that's lacking now is a letter from the dead man himself! he thought.

The envelope seemed weighty, but he decided it could not be otherwise for a letter from a widow. What is she saying? he wondered. What news do you have for us, Comrade Clytemnestra? . . .

"Burn it!" his wife said, matter-of-factly.

In the silent room, the familiar noise of a match being struck could be heard quite clearly, followed by the hungry flame and then its extinction. The faint crackling sound of carbonised paper went on for a while.

He waited for his wife to have left with the ash-tray before he said to the secretary, "I don't want her to send me any more letters. She shouldn't even think of writing."

He did not want to know what had gone on in that house. How they had striven, then taken fresh counsel, whether they had delayed, or screamed in the fog. Let them take it all to the grave with them!

The secretary's heavy breathing told him the latter was about to make an observation. Maybe about the storks' nest. For no reason, he suddenly recalled a swarthy Greek who answered to the name of Haxhi,[*]

*Albanian "xh" is pronounced like the English "dg" in "badge." The Greek's name thus sounds like *hajj*, the pilgrimage to Mecca.

159

and the kids in the street who taunted him with the refrain: *Haxhi, haxhibird, when are you going to fly off to Mecca?*

Nowadays he often felt drowsy at this time of day.

2

The Central Committee plenum had begun on the stroke of four in the afternoon, and the first session was still going on. Dusk was coming on. The Guide had his elbows on the table, and he could feel the meeting going slack. He could imagine the questioning glances going around among the delegates. They had been expecting a dramatic meeting; they had probably only managed snatches of sleep before first light, but the agenda was going on and on with items that were frankly insipid. Questions of raising the budget for the energy sector and extending the schedule for fulfilling the Plan. Those who had been afraid were presumably enjoying it; long may this last, they must have been thinking; let's keep on about hydroelectric generators, cotton plantations, the emancipation of women . . . Whereas others, who couldn't wait to hear the crack of the whip, sank by stages into ill humour. The big secrets, the secrets that would make your hair stand on end, were probably only dealt with in the inner sanctum, in the Politburo, whereas they got the donkeywork: budgets, five-year plans and so on . . .

When he'd entered the room, Adrian Hasobeu was ashen-faced. Head hung low, he'd gone to sit in the fourth row back; the adjacent seats stayed empty. The Guide learned these details from words whispered in his ear by the new Successor-designate, who for the first time was seated on the leader's right-hand side.

He'd stopped taking interest in the audience, but after the break, when they had all come back to their seats and his freshly appointed Successor had informed him that there were now not four but six vacant seats around Hasobeu, the Guide's resentment of his minister, as black as any long-buried rancour returning to life from the tomb, became unbearable.

"Dog!" he muttered under his breath.

There he was sitting on his own like a leper, but still he would not listen to reason!

The plenum had moved on to the second item on the agenda. When the first secretary of the Tirana branch of the Party had finished his speech, Hasobeu requested permission to speak. Each time he brought the microphone nearer to his mouth his voice grew more feeble. The Guide didn't stop staring hard at the man's blank and clouded eyes. But when Hasobeu got around to talking about the great conspiracy, he interrupted him:

"We've heard what you had to say, Comrade. You've told us about the twenty years you spent as minister of the interior, and so on and so forth. But since you've just mentioned the conspiracy, I'd like to ask you a question: why have all conspiracies unmasked to this day been discovered by the Party, not by the *Sigurimi* — which was under your command, wasn't it?"

Since he could not see him, he could easily imagine Hasobeu holding on tight to the desk so as not to collapse, then grasping the microphone, and getting tangled up in the wire looping around him like a snake.

Prowling hyena! he raged silently. Snake in the grass!

Hasobeu had made an attempt to reply, but shuffling in the hall drowned out the sound of his words.

"Throttle the man once and for all!" the Guide snarled to himself.

He hadn't expected his spite for the man to surge up quite so vigorously. At times it was on the point of taking his breath away.

A seventeen-year-old girl had committed suicide

because a mere bicycle repairman had dropped her.

"You got the message too, didn't you? That I didn't love you anymore!" he growled under his breath.

Hasobeu ought to have seen the light as far back as last winter. Later on as well, and then again in the last few days. So what had he been waiting for? Had the Guide's cold shoulder not sufficed to make him vanish into thin air? Did a bicycle repairman have more power than *Himself*? It made you want to tear your hair out.

From the back of the room someone shouted, "Hasobeu, stop shilly-shallying!"

"Throttle the man," he mumbled again as he silenced the brouhaha with a wave of his hand.

You're going to force me to set the black beast on you, he thought.

That was the name that he rather strangely gave to the intermediate night, the one he sometimes inserted between two sessions of the same plenum.

The suspended night was his own invention. It stifled like oakum. Everyone could feel it looming, but no one would dare admit it.

With the hand that he used to call for order, he now pulled on his watch chain.

He'd fingered the same ice-cold chain thirty years before, barely realising what terror he was about to unleash. "Comrades, since it is getting late . . ."

Over the years, the silence at meetings had grown deeper.

Even before he had finished speaking, he felt the familiar thrill rippling around the room before washing back over him. He tarried a moment, until he had his full measure of it. The unending calm that followed that kind of ecstasy had no equal. Except maybe in distant regions of sleep, under other skies.

There was no need for a sharp-beaked eagle or for a clap of thunder. Both would emerge from the ensuing night.

At him, boy! At him! he thought affectionately as he rose to leave the hall.

3

He found it difficult to sleep. The first interruption left him only half awake, weighed down by some kind of impossibility. One way or another he would have liked to reward Hasobeu, but he just could not work out what to do with his ice-cold corpse or with the bullet wound in his forehead, which looked more than real, as if it had been painted on. The second time he awoke, just before dawn, it was as if, while washing according to ancient custom under the porch of a minaret, he had been suddenly beset by a question: couldn't they have found someone else to do this job? A gypsy looking on said, "Don't get so worked up, it's what people have been doing for generations in your father's family." He meant to answer back: That's a libel put out by the émigré press! — but the words wouldn't come.

When he woke up in the morning, he recalled fragments of these meanderings and his mood darkened. If his mother had still been alive, she would have remonstrated: you only suffer those nightmares since you banned the Muslim faith!

As usual, his wife was waiting for him at the breakfast table. As soon as he caught her glance he knew there was no news on the Hasobeu front.

Snake! he thought. Impotent little goat!

As he sipped his coffee, he felt the emptiness in his breast increasing alongside the impression that something had been lost forever.

"I wouldn't have expected this of him," he mused.

The euphoria that had welled up inside him the day before had been replaced by an anxiety that was difficult to pinpoint.

His wife looked at her watch.

He shook his head. What had been done could not be undone. "Just wait, you'll soon find out who you're up against," he mumbled, and then left the table.

By the time he walked into the assembly room an hour later, he had convinced himself that no one had ever treated him with more brazen treachery than Adrian Hasobeu. He had flaunted his disrespect as openly as a flag on a masthead. So you expected me to commit suicide during the night between the two sessions? To follow in the footsteps of Kano Zhbira, Omer Shejnan and the Successor?

For the time being Hasobeu was sitting on his own, as on the previous day, with a similarly ashen face, but visibly delighted by his defiant gesture.

The Guide imagined him being shot on the banks of some waterway in the northern suburbs of the city and being left unburied, but even then he didn't feel at ease. He would have managed to pass on his evil before leaving this world. The stalwart black-haired beast, the intermediate night, would have ended up yielding to him. That would have been his final mission.

Maybe it was his own fault, he thought wearily. He shouldn't have worked the beast so hard. For all the terror it cast, it was a delicate thing.

The hush in the hall told him that the assembled delegates were waiting for him to speak.

"It's Comrade Hasobeu's turn to take the floor," he growled.

Hasobeu didn't stay at the microphone for long. When a disapproving rumble rippled through the room, the Guide didn't bother to mask his fury, and broke in:

"We told you yesterday already: Stop prevaricating, Hasobeu! That's the last warning."

Two minutes later, the Guide interrupted him again:

"Listen here, you swamp-fly!"

As he choked on his words, his Successor nudged a glass of water toward him.

He drank the contents of the glass, tried to go on, but because he was so upset, he still couldn't get his voice to obey him.

The audience had turned to stone. Never before had such wrath been expressed in word or gesture by the Guide. His eyes shone with such supernatural brilliance that, according to later accounts of the scene, many of those present thought he had recovered his sight. First they felt like applauding him, then they fell into silent lamentation, then joy regained the upper hand. Oh Guide, Oh our leader, tell us what irks thee! they pleaded in their minds. Tell us all you know about that Judas, even if it's hard for you. Feed us the poison with your own hand, watch us writhing in pain like chimeras, watch us fall on one another, tearing our neighbours' flesh with our teeth; then, as breath leaves us, crawl to your feet and lie there until we die.

Hasobeu had also frozen stiff on the platform. His jaw opened as if to form words, but an invisible vice clamped it shut. Hunched over the lectern, hanging onto it to stop himself from falling over, he finally managed to blurt out, "I — am — not — guilty!"

Glued to the lectern, with death in his eyes, he could hear shouts from all sides: "Traitor! String him up!" and immediately saw hands shoot up to vote in favour of expelling him from the Party.

Before he had quite recovered his senses he heard people saying, "Out you go!" As he walked toward the exit, he noticed the membership secretary standing in

his way. He couldn't make out what the man was saying to him, or what he meant by pointing toward the
left side of his chest, where his heart was. His numbed
mind was still able to reflect that, however much the
man might have sharpened his nails, he wouldn't
manage to snatch out his heart with bare hands. But
as he thought that thought, the man was putting his
fingers inside Hasobeu's jacket and into the inside
pocket right next to his heart, whence he extracted
the ex-minister's Party card.

The feet that fell on the broad, red-carpeted steps
seemed no longer his own. Now that his Party card
had been confiscated, he was halfway to his death
already.

He had already gone down many steps, but the
stairway seemed endless. The cloakroom right at the
bottom looked tiny, as if it were buried in some deep
abyss, and the few staff seemed like so many dwarves.

When he finally made it to the cloakroom, one of
the concierges took down a coat and brought it to
him, holding it up with both hands. His expression
was devoid of hostility. They looked each other in the
eye for a good while. Not only were the concierge's
eyes entirely unaggressive, they were sparkling with

unspoken thoughts. And the hands that helped Hasobeu into his overcoat were as respectful of him as they had ever been.

Are the people upstairs in the know? he wondered privately. To tell the truth, he didn't quite understand the meaning of his own question. It got mixed up with other questions, while the concierge whispered in his ear, "Pull yourself together, boss!"

He was stroking Hasobeu's aching back, not even seeking to mask his long-standing faithfulness and devotion.

It took the merest fraction of a second, as short as a flash of lightning, to realise that the tempest of anger that the Guide had unleashed on him upstairs could not possibly have been without cause, and that without knowing it, without even wanting it, he, Hasobeu, had probably been, for ages already, at the helm of a great conspiracy.

His supporters, unable to repress their veneration any longer, were about to proclaim him *Prijs*.

No! he meant to cry out. Though they had both trampled on him, he would never betray the Party or the Guide.

"No!" he shouted as he tried to disentangle himself from his cursed overcoat. He had but one wish now — to rush up those stairs, to burst into the hall, and to proclaim the news: the other conspirators, my henchmen, are downstairs; they're waiting for you with long capes drenched in blood and dirt, the better to wrap you in!

He shifted his shoulders to try to get properly free from these sly glances, but the concierge's grip grew firmer and he found himself held tight, as in a vice. The man's assistant, who had been calmly observing the scene, stepped forward, and with a deft movement of his arm took the handcuffs out of his pocket and snapped them on.

4

The fall of Adrian Hasobeu was greeted in Tirana with more indifference than scorn.

As soon as they heard it said that "Hasobeu has fallen", city folk, as if waking from a snooze, recalled that his fate, like the Successor's, had always been known. The only difference between the two cases was that whereas the fall of the Successor had taken but a single season, Hasobeu's had begun a year before, or rather no, not a year, but six years, or even more, say sixteen years, or maybe even twenty years ago, when he'd been appointed commander-in-chief of the *Sigurimi*. His fall and its cause were obvious: he'd had access to secrets.

News came quickly from Tirana's prison that as soon as he had been taken in Hasobeu had had his tongue cut out, which proved how dangerous those secrets would have been had they been let out, even in the form of screams echoing between the four walls of a prison cell.

A persistent rumour sprang up in the capital at that time, as if to fill the silence left by Hasobeu's sectioned tongue. But to everyone's surprise, the rumour soon detached itself from Hasobeu and became refocused on the Successor, before being entirely swallowed up by the latter's unfathomable enigma.

That was when it became apparent that the mystery of the Successor would emerge as the victor and would occupy a position that the unhappy man had never managed to gain in life: that of being at the top, or, as people had taken to saying in recent times, of being "Number One".

His long-deserted residence, where no light had shone for ages, could still just about be made out through the foliage lining the Grand Boulevard.

Passersby, especially late-nighters on the way home from the National Theatre after watching some self-congratulatory play full of vulgar laughs and noble feelings, were always seized by a shiver of fear that they would not have missed for anything in the world. It must presumably have been one such person who, on coming out of a show, suggested that the deserted residence was precisely where Europe began — an idea that got him called in a few hours later, in the middle of the night, to explain what he had said. At first he tried to wriggle out of it, claiming what he'd more or less meant to say was that that was where the conspiracy had started, that's to say the curse of Albania, or in other words its perdition, until, during the third day of torture, he confessed that he was against social-ist realism, that it was indeed his disrespect for it that had led him to have such a twisted idea because, if it had been in his power, he would have shut down the National Theatre because it could not compete in any way with the Elizabethan residence of the Successor, the only building in Albania to have some degree of resemblance to the castles and baroque palaces of Europe.

It was a fact that the gloomy dwelling aroused increasing numbers of crazy fantasies and all kinds of fevered emotions. On that December night the dead man, his wife and Hasobeu had paced untiringly around it, inside and out. They had made signals to each other, had sought to interpret them, as in a mime show, but they dealt with something on which they appeared not to agree. Maybe the lightning had obscured the light of the lantern that was supposed to be a signal from someone inside to someone waiting outside, or perhaps it was the opposite, someone outside signalling to someone in the house.

To this whirligig of wraiths a fourth character was added by a patient in the Tirana Psychiatric Hospital. The architect. Although he had long familiarity with these kinds of delusions, the doctor who first heard the man was dumbstruck. What was an artist with white-skinned hands doing in this murky imbroglio? With hands that only moved to take a pencil and give life to lines that in their very subtlety only served to tie everyone else in knots?

That was the doctor's first thought, but on further reflection he saw that it was only to be expected that in such a mysterious house, with all its deceptive signs and doorways, the miraculous role of the architect must have been essential to the unfolding of the whole story.

Meanwhile, at the start of that winter, questions about the true story of the Successor's fall, about which hand — his own or another's — had shortened his life, swirled around more furiously than ever.

As could have been foreseen, clairvoyants, who had been lying low for a time, made a comeback. The most persistent was the Icelander. He had started by establishing contact with the denizen of the Other-world, whose death rattle was now just as awful as before, and his story just as murky. He was complaining about something missing, perhaps referring to a part of his body, but he might also have meant a part of his faculties.

As a result, apart from the presence of the two women, who were still there, if only very faintly, behind what the clairvoyant called a "curtain of snow", the rest of it seemed impossible to interpret. It was especially hard to understand what connected the Successor to these two women, just as it was not easy, not to say impossible, to explain the squabble and the blame-casting that was going on between them. As before, the recriminations sounded like pleading, to be sure, but they also were just as much reminiscent of commands or bawling. Someone's death was being demanded. But whose? And from whom?

In other circumstances, commentators would have sneered as in the old days: sentimental nonsense about wives wanting to get rid of a mistress, or vice versa, and so on, but the end of that week had been exhausting, and nobody was in the mood to laugh. With the weariness induced by having said it all before, one of the analysts suggested that, in addition to the two by now well-known hypotheses — an attempt to enlarge the Atlantic alliance to southeastern Europe, on the one hand, and the discovery of new oilfields off the Albanian coastline — the Icelandic clairvoyant's opinion was that you could not rule out the possibility that the events of the night of December 13 had involved one of the members of the family.

SIX

THE ARCHITECT

When one morning in early spring — the whole city was still striving without success to solve the puzzle of the most mysterious death of the period — when on that morning in March I confessed to my wife that I was the killer, the poor woman must surely have thought I had gone out of my mind.

On getting up, I noticed tear-streaks on her cheek, but neither then nor ever after, not even now that my name belongs to the list of shadows on patrol around the residence on the night of December 13, did she or I broach the subject again.

Now and again, just before making love, at those moments when the impossible seems within reach, I notice a little glimmer in her eyes, a twinkle suggesting curiosity, and I expect her to ask: what came over you the other day to make you tell such a crazy story? But she remains silent, presumably out of fear that the question itself would bring the craziness back into being.

One evening, thirsting to confess, I took the initiative and said, "Do you remember when in the half-light I told you that I . . . that it was I who . . . ," she put her hand over my mouth and wouldn't let me finish the sentence. Pain and entreaty were writ so large on her face that I swore to myself I would never again yield to temptation.

So now I am condemned forever more to turn all these things over in my mind alone. What things? Questions and hypotheses, hers and other people's.

Sometimes I resent her for this. She is certainly entitled to believe I am not the murderer. But all the same, she was in a better position than anybody else to sense my crime. For she was the only person who knew about the humiliation I suffered at the hand of the Successor, about my anger with him and my sudden need for revenge.

It all arose at the first, last and only luncheon party I was invited to at his house, to mark the launch of the remodelling project. I don't recall which joke of mine or of the son's managed to irritate the master of the house. The wine we had been drinking made us tipsy and we had probably uttered words that could be called sophomoric. Looking daggers at me with his icy stare, he riposted that liberal brains such as ours might find cooperative cow barns more profitable than studying for diplomas.

That was enough to make us all sober up instantly. The humiliation he had inflicted made me profoundly resentful. Under his own roof, in this great residence that I was about to transform into an object of beauty, he dared to threaten me, the architect, with mucking out cattle on a cooperative farm! As I plodded home, resentment boiled over into rage. The anger was hot and unprecedented, it seemed to be coming from various spirits that had come to inhabit my body.

I felt breathless even as I sauntered along the banks of the Lana. My fury, far from subsiding, grew only worse, becoming blind and violent, and was already beginning to merge into a thirst for revenge.

I was beside myself. I was clearly suffering some kind of sudden madness. The feeling that this could not be just a matter of an offended luncheon guest experiencing a fit of anger but had to come from a longer-standing resentment passed through my mind once again. The entire mass of certain other former architects' rancour weighed heavily on my heart. All those abuses inflicted at the foot of the pyramids, forty centuries ago — hands cut off, eyes put out. Screams percolating from the dungeons in the Tower of London. The moaning of Minos, the inventor of the fearsome Labyrinth. Pleas made to the palace of the Atrides. To the palace of Ceausescu . . .

Everyone was crying out for vengeance in a land where, after reigning for a thousand years, the ancient Customary Law of the *Kanun* had just been buried. Moreover, all my predecessors expected it from me, their great-great-grandson in misfortune, bereft of the arms or the courage to do justice to them.

What could I do, except make the renovation as ugly as possible?

I was the first to be taken aback by this additional fit of madness . . .

A ghastly residence . . . I felt like bursting out laughing at this petty vengeance, but it made me immediately want to burst into tears. When I got home, my wife blanched as soon as she saw me. "What are you saying, my darling sparrow?" she said over and over, as I told her what had happened. Imagining the worst, as was her wont, she could already see us deported to a muddy outpost, with me shovelling dung and she milking goats.

As always when this kind of thing happened, we ended up in bed. We moaned a lot louder than my persecuted predecessors.

Later on, we had coffee and tried to calm each other down. "You thought of making a mess of the residence, didn't you?" she asked, without managing to laugh. I begged her not to nag me about that again. I promised her that if I was not taken off the job I would make the house the most beautiful residence in the whole of Albania. If they let me, I said more than once, if only they let me get on with it . . .

I worried for a whole week until a telephone call from the department responsible for state apartments made me understand that there had been no change in the assignment.

I felt resurrected, and had all the trouble in the world waiting until the next dawn to get to my studio. Grades, angles and drafts seemed just as eager to jump back into my hands. In an instant they seemed to have joined together in a kind of inner harmony. To such an extent that I often had the impression that during the night, while I was sleeping, they were quietly getting on with putting on finishing touches themselves. It lasted two whole days. My two assistants didn't hide their amazement. They now whispered, "A masterpiece!" without the slightest fear that they might be suspected of toadying. During the afternoon coffee break, we often said nothing, but it was obvious that our thoughts were revolving in common around the work at hand.

It was on just such an afternoon, in the midst of a silence pulsating with emotion, that I almost shouted out loud, "You idiot!" To judge by the expression on my assistants' faces, I could see I must have been smiling in that foolish way my wife found so appalling, for she knew that it was my means of dissimulating and hiding secrets. Remembering my brief fit of stupid hate, when I had thought of making an unholy mess of the remodelling project, I almost burst into guffaws. That might in fact have been what I was gearing up to do spontaneously, without further reflection, but suddenly something switched, as if there had been an eclipse. An icy wind blew in from the distant past and suddenly enveloped me with an idea I had heard spoken of somewhere or other: in architecture as in all other domains, it is not ugliness, but its opposite, beauty, that can be fatal.

Six royal stallions . . .

It was the voice of my Hungarian teacher telling us a tale from days of yore, a story about a king of France envying one of his vassals for his splendid château. It all came back to me with astonishing precision. *Six royal stallions at full gallop through the dark of night . . .* Words spoken twenty-five years ago echoed in my ears as if they had been uttered just yesterday; similarly, I could feel myself sinking back into the drowsiness induced by the overheated classroom in the Budapest Architecture School. The vassal had not only had the cheek to have a castle built that was even finer than the king's, but he had invited his monarch to its inauguration party.

Királyi hatos fogat,* six of the king's horses, at full gallop they rode . . .

I wanted to get it out of my mind but I could not.

Three hours after midnight, his face twisted by rage, the king and his escort set off at a gallop for Paris.

"Are you feeling okay?" one of my assistants asked.

I must have acknowledged the question some way

*In Hungarian in the original.

183

or other. The thought that it was the overweening vassal and not the architect who had been punished began to soothe my spirit a little. Yes, it was the vassal, a kind of Successor, who had been struck down for having dared to compete with the monarch . . .

As I sipped my second cup of coffee, it struck me that the memory had probably not come back to the surface by mere chance. Incomplete snatches of sentences, evasive glances, and awkward silences swirled around in my mind like a cloud of dust suddenly brought into focus by a shaft of sunlight . . . This residence is beginning to look splendid . . . It's unbelievably handsome . . . Maybe even more handsome than . . . more beautiful than . . . than the . . .

The light of their lanterns scouring the dark canopy of trees, the royal six-in-hand raced along at breakneck speed, drawing ever nearer to Paris. Inside the coach, where it was darker than night, the monarch mulled over the revenge he was about to mete out to his vassal.

"*Khaany mori zurgaan,*" I said under my breath, mechanically reciting the phrase my professor had taught me, not in Hungarian but in Mongol. It was one of those jokes that generate spontaneously in a circle of students and then spread all the more easily for their complete zaniness. It had started right after the class, as we were going into the canteen for lunch. Jan, the Slovak in the class, put on the professor's voice and called out from afar to the waitress, "I'll have a royal six-in-hand with mashed potatoes, please!" We all burst out laughing, but the laughter turned to applause when Cong, our Mongolian comrade, a normally very shy fellow, took up the refrain and bellowed, "I'll have a royal six-in-hand too, thank you very much!" . . . Amid the general hilarity, the inevitable happened: we asked our Mongolian to give us the same quotation in his native language, and that's the bizarre reason why the celebrated line became part of the folklore of the Architecture School in Mongol: *khaany mori zurgaan.*

"How about a bit of fresh air?" one of my assistants shyly suggested.

As we walked I felt more and more uneasy. I was in a hurry to get back inside the studio so as to look over the drawings again.

An ill light seemed to be falling on them now.

I tried to reassure myself. It was a different age, full of whimsical kings and madcap vassals. But a small voice inside me said the opposite: regimes change, as do customs and cathedrals, but crimes are ever the same. And envy, the prime though oft-forgotten mover of crime, doesn't fade away but grows ever blacker.

I kept my eyes glued to the drawings. I had never thought before then that a murder could be seen in that way. As I picked up my ruler and pencil it was as if I was taking hold of the tools of crime. I kept telling myself: it is still in your power to avoid a fatal outcome. You can still make these blades into instruments of salvation, like the surgeon's knife.

Well, that's what I thought . . . All I needed to do was to touch up the blueprint. To spoil the proportions, to destroy the inner harmony. In a word: to mess it up.

I was besieged by thoughts of that kind especially at night. At the hour of pity, as I nicknamed it. Stop shilly-shallying! Go on, save one life, or rather, the lives of a whole family, and maybe hundreds of other lives as well.

At such times it seemed that my mind was made up. But in the light of the new day, my other inclination, my evil side, had no trouble reasserting itself. Apparently, aesthetic beauty had no truck with pity. It got on rather better with Death than its opposite.

Once again I tried to find reassurance. That old story had taken place more than three hundred years earlier. It was a different period, there was private property, laws weren't the same as now. However, that didn't stop me in any way from having a clear vision of the king of France's anger, and I could see him in the pale light of dawn, all bespattered with the dirt of the journey, drawing up the decree laying down his vassal's sentence. And as one thing leads to another, I could envision the Guide's resentment of his Successor. In his own lifetime, he dared to build, barely a few paces away, a finer residence than his own. It wouldn't be difficult to imagine how large his statue would be after his death.

As soon as I got back to the studio with my head spinning from these thoughts, I pored over the architectural drawings to get down to work. I took out a balcony, I shortened two pillars, but instead of spoiling the villa as I intended, the changes only added to the perfection of the plans.

Had anyone known my inner turmoil, he or she would presumably have accused me of being petty-minded, of attempting by underhand means to take revenge for the offence suffered at that now far-off luncheon with the Successor.

May my soul be witness to the fact that the offence had long been expunged from my heart. What was happening could be ascribed to anything you like, save to that episode.

Something quite different was at stake. Something a thousand times more secret and by the same token far more painful. It was my own hell, which I had sworn to divulge to no living being, to my dying day. That pain had to do with art. I had betrayed it. By my own hand I had stifled my own talent. We all did the same, and for the most part we all had the same excuse for our contempt of art: the times we lived in.

It was our collective alibi, our smokescreen, our wickedness. There was socialist realism, indisputably; there were laws, actually not so much law as a reign of terror, but in spite of all that, we could have drawn at least a few harmonious lines, even if only haphazardly, as in a dream. But our fingers were all thumbs, because our souls were bound.

I was probably one of the few who asked themselves the fateful question: do I or do I not possess any talent? Was it the age that had turned my hands into clay, or was I so clumsy that I would have vegetated no matter what period I lived in — in the capitalist era, in the feudal age, at the end of paganism, at the dawn of Christianity, in the Paleolithic, under the Inquisition, or at the time of post-Impressionism? Would I not have exclaimed and lamented in all and any age that I would have been a great artist but for Pharaoh Thutmose blocking my gifts, but for Caligula, but for McCarthy, but for Zhdanov . . .

When at the end of a storm-tossed afternoon I poured my heart out to my wife, she replied with tears in her eyes, "If you are going through such pain, you must be unlike the others."

Perhaps I am . . . In what looked like an unending wasteland, she planted the first seed of hope.

At that luncheon with the Successor, alongside humiliation I felt a vague, as yet ill-defined foreboding of fame. Of course I was offended . . . but at the sovereign's table. Like my illustrious predecessors who dined with Nero, with the ruler of the Middle Empire, with Stalin, with Kubla Khan. They too had been threatened with relegation.

Later on, when the fear of punishment had subsided and I was back in the studio, I felt not that my hands were even more tied, but the opposite. Something seemed to have been released inside me. That freeing suddenly made me feel I had jumped over the rainbow, a fantasy we had as children when we imagined that was how boys could turn into little girls and girls could become boys.

What I actually felt was that I had taken a step of much greater import: I had escaped from the desert of mediocrity. That was the straw I clutched at, and it kept me afloat.

Absorbed as I was by the beauty of the planned remodelling, I lost track of all those thoughts. Sometimes when I looked over the drawings I said to myself: this is the residence of a Communist sovereign. A private dwelling in a country where collective property is the rule. An androgynous building half built under the monarchy, and half built now. That's why it had such a foreign look, like something from very far away. Like a dream.

All the same, the royal six-in-hand frequently galloped through my mind. I did my best not to pay it any attention. I owed accounts only to my art. The rest was none of my business.

I was well aware I had taken a dangerous gamble.

I was convinced I was putting up a temple that would be crowned by mourning. As the saying goes, something to die for . . .

An inner voice urged: if you want to save the master of the house and his relatives, hold back and give in to mediocrity. But the other voice answered back: they've got nothing to do with you; art is your vocation, its laws alone you should obey. Even if your art engenders murder, your hands will be clean. There is no art without grieving. Which is precisely what constitutes its sombre greatness.

It was at about the same time that I first heard of the underground passageway. To begin with, it prompted a feeling of great relief. So a murder plan had already been around, unconnected to me or my remodelling project. Independently of my proposals, someone had thought that the murderers ought to have a secret passageway available to them, for surreptitious entry into the building. It wasn't me who had thought of it, it was someone else.

The relief was short-lived. I quickly recalled that the rumour had been reported to me by the Successor's son. It was probably his own imagination, presumably the fruit of his curious ponderings on the ties between the two leaders. He talked about them in a bizarre way, calling them ties of blood, and he even went so far as to compare the tunnel to an umbilical cord.

However, even if they sprang from an exuberant imagination, these wild suggestions were very pertinent to my plan. It was not by chance that they had arisen at the same time as the remodelling project. However much I tried to keep the rumours at a distance, the tunnel was part of the project. Everything was dependent on it. It would be by my order alone that murderers would use it. *A parancsomra ök gyilkolhatnak . . .** At my command they will kill . . .

These notions buzzed around in my head for days on end. It became something as repetitive as boredom. I had the fate of a whole clan in my hands. All I had to do was to make a mess of the dwelling and the murderers would have to stay crouching in the tunnel for centuries. Otherwise . . .

The days sped by. The work was nearing completion. The residence was still hidden by scaffolding. It seemed to me that everyone was waiting impatiently for it to be dismantled so as to reveal the new residence.

September was on us, and the leaves began to fall quietly. The scaffolding was taken down at night, a few days before the engagement party. All around, silence reigned.

When on the day of the party, that Sunday afternoon, I crossed the threshold, the other guests were already there. I wasn't at ease in the glowing atmosphere, joyous and relaxed. Suzana, in her pale

---

*In Hungarian in the original.

dress, seemed the incarnation of harmony and proportion.

Good wishes were on everyone's lips. May there be only happiness under this roof! Who's the architect? Ah, so you're the architect. Congratulations, a thousand congratulations, what a gem!

After my second glass of champagne, I almost screamed out: talk about whatever you want, but not about this house! We can do without your comments, close your eyes, for pity's sake!

But it was too late. The assassins had already taken up their quarters, underneath, in the dark, lower down than even the foundations of the house. A *parancsot nem lehet megtagadni* . . . The order could not be countermanded . . .

A final glimmer of hope lit my heart when I saw the Guide's blank stare. Though he was trying hard to mask them, the first signs of blindness were apparent. He can't see a thing, I thought, he's in no position to make anything out at all clearly. In spite of myself, I imagined him prowling around the house with shuffling gait feeling the walls with his hands, as the blind do in order to form an idea of things or people. But touch does not allow you to tell the beautiful from the ugly.

That's what I was thinking until the hope I nurtured was dashed to the ground as I saw the look of his wife standing at his side. Her narrowed, sarcastic eyes were scrutinising everything, down to the smallest detail. I thought: it would have been better if his were still the seeing eyes, not hers. I never found out what happened right after the ceremony, when the Guide left with his wife.

Khaany mori zurgaan . . . He didn't need a six-in-hand or a coach. It was not a long way from one house to the other, from the Guide's to the Successor's. But it was far enough.

SEVEN

THE SUCCESSOR

Mediums and masters of the occult, you know the mysteries and the paths that lead to them. Nonetheless I say to you again, for the thousandth time: leave me in peace! Even if I wanted, I could not give you what you seek. It is not transmissible, not because of any whim on my part, nor because of any incompetence on yours, but because it is so by its very nature.

I am other. What's more, I am not whole. I have no grave, and I am lacking half my skull. I have been exhumed so often — lugged here and there, flung unceremoniously into sacks and plastic bags with lumps of earth and shingle — that part of me has gone missing. But that's a mere detail. Even if I were whole, even if I had been embalmed and preserved in a marble tomb, you would not get anything out of me besides fog and chaos.

I am other in a different sense. I am of infinite otherness, such that each link in my otherness engenders another kind of otherness, which in turn engenders another, and so on, which prevents all understanding between us.

I was the *Pasardhës*. He who comes next. But nextness was not a question of distance, such as the two paces I had to leave between us when standing behind the Guide as we paraded onto the platform or stood on the rostrum. Nor was it a chronological nextness, referring to the years I would reign after him. No, it was a much more complicated business.

We are a race apart, and we can only understand each other. But we are so few in number that amid the dark turmoil of this world above which human souls swirl, it is only rarely, extremely rarely — once every thousand years, maybe every ten thousand? — that we ever come across one of our own.

Thus, one summer's night, I saw a scorched silhouette fleeing all alone, and thought I glimpsed my opposite number Lin Biao, the designated successor of Mao Zedong. But it can't have been him, apparently, as he didn't return my greeting. Or perhaps he didn't recognise me, because you can't argue that someone graced as I am with only half a head is more recognisable than a burnt-out skeleton.

I was really sorry to miss that opportunity to exchange a few words with a colleague. To tell each other about our respective enigmas, or at least to share feelings about our fates: have you seen what they've done to us! My need was so strong that I turned my head, but meanwhile it had become impossible to pinpoint him in the celestial vault. My only solace was the thought that the opportunity to meet again would perhaps recur in the next two or twelve thousand years.

To him, a man of my own kind, I could have told the story of what happened to me; but no way can I tell you. For unlike the language that serves for us to talk to one another, a language allowing our kind to communicate with yours has not yet been invented on earth, and never will be.

That's why we can never agree on any subject. That's why the suspicions that beset me on that night of December 13 remain vivid and topical despite Albania's subsequent transformation. We could have more easily imagined the ground changing place with the sky than we could have foreseen the country's turnaround. But in the end, Albania did turn. However, despite that upheaval my puzzle, or rather, the double enigma of the Guide and myself, remains unresolved. Nothing has helped to solve it: the opening of the archives, the belated autopsies, the identification of my remains, clairvoyants from Alaska, the Kremlin, and the Accursed Mountains, even Mossad — no thing or person has made a dent in the shield that protects our secret.

The same questions will not stop nagging through the ages. What happened on the night of December 13? What caused the Successor to fall? Who pulled the trigger?

That night . . . Ah, how impossible it is to explain anything about it! The night, to begin with. Was there a night of December 13? Hard to say. I was lying on my bed, drifting toward sleep, waiting for my wife to bring me another cup of chamomile tea. Now and again she wandered toward the window as if trying to spy something outside in the dark. I was half asleep, and in my mind I was already in the assembly room where I was to appear the next day, answering the same questions. The place I would be a few hours later, but not in flesh and blood, only in spirit. They were discussing me as if I were still alive, with the

Guide barely succeeding in holding back his tears: And now that you are back among us after this terrible shock, dear Comrade Successor, make yourself vital to the Party once again!

When I was already in the morgue, they behaved as if nothing had happened, as if there had been no night of December 13, but instead, a different set of events, a kind of parallel sequence, some unnatural cut-and-paste of the day before and the day after that stopped time flowing between them. Or made it flow in reverse.

Anyone else would have found this reversal bizarre. But not I. It was part of my being, in its essence as well as its outward form.

My life in no way resembled human living. Such cases are often called "a dog's life". It was worse than that. It was a Successor's life. I was he who would come after. Preassigned to fill the Guide's shoes. Which was how he reminded us all, but himself first of all, that one day he would not be there anymore, whereas I would go on existing.

Some days, the thought of it terrified me. I wondered how he could bear it himself. How could he tolerate my being there, how could he tolerate all the others who had accepted the pact? Why didn't he rise up and shout: what on earth makes you think the future course of events can be known with such certainty? Why are we looking to the grave to order current affairs? Was it so exceptional for mortals to die in defiance of the established order? Why in his case, or rather in both our cases, was this order to be treated as the bottom line, at any price?

At times when I felt less tense with anxiety, I was sorry for the man. I swooned with the affection that his generosity inspired. I was prepared to throw myself at his feet and implore him: *Prijs*, if you have the slightest misgiving, take the title away from me, yes, take back the title! Sometimes I went even further and told him in my heart: Ask what you will, we are all prepared to lay down our lives for you. Gives us an opportunity to show these are not just vain words. And this time let me have the first turn. At the dark hour, when death is nigh, give me your leave to take the final step and, by leaving my place and my mortal coil, to stare death in the eye by laying down my life on your behalf.

I knew I meant it. Maybe even more than I should have, as on that April night when we were hanging around together on the balcony after dining. We'd been discussing events of the past, in particular when we'd broken off certain relations. We'd got on to the falling out with China when, taking a deep breath, he blurted out that it was rumoured that Lin Biao, Mao's successor, hadn't been a traitor and certainly hadn't been burned to a crisp in the airplane in which he was trying to escape — but that Mao had had him to dinner and then had him killed when the meal was over.

I have no idea how long I stood there like a statue! All I know is that each split second that passed seemed unbearable, because of all the dangerous conversation topics we could have touched on, that was by the far the worst. Unthinkingly I came out with a "You never know . . ." Just to make matters worse, I went on to say that I didn't believe he was guilty any more than I thought him innocent.

He stared at me with deep feeling. Then he got up from the sofa and came over to put his arm around me. His chest was heaving with sobs as he murmured softly, "You are the most loyal, the most faithful among the faithful." His cheek wet with tears pressed against mine, but suddenly a question seared my heart. What was all this weeping about? Had I not deceived myself? Had I not sealed my fate with my own words? Was he in fact mourning me before my departure?

That night I couldn't sleep a wink. I kept fixating on his sobs and tears, which seemed to have only one explanation: he had been moved by my sincerity. I had said what I thought without imagining that my own suspicion of treason on the part of the Chinese successor could amount to an unwitting confession of a similar sentiment buried deep inside my unconscious mind. I talked myself down in that way but a contrary thought sprang up in immediate response: hadn't I gone too far with sincerity? Hadn't I hoisted myself on my own petard? For days on end I tried to make out what he really thought of me, but I never picked up the slightest sequel to that after-dinner talk. I guessed he must have forgotten it. His brain needed to lose ballast, just like anyone else's. I came to understand, only a little too late, that I was wrong. He never forgot anything.

When my hour came, with the night of December 13 and then the day of December 14, when he stopped time in its track, only then did I grasp for a brief instant that by turning back the hands on the clock he had only restored things to their proper order. An order that in his mind had been undone when, as legends tell us, father and son mistake their places for each other's.

He was racked by sobbing when he gave a speech I was no longer there to hear, just as he had been the previous April during that moment after dinner when, perhaps for the first time, he had come to the conclusion I had knowingly signed my own death warrant.

Most people might have thought the Guide's sentimentality mere playacting, but I was in a better position than anyone else to know the truth. Those sobs were completely genuine. You can't understand that, just as you can't understand so much else. You find it hard to realise that in this world, he and I hated each other even while we loved each other, and conversely, we adored each other even as each deplored the other. Especially on days like that December 14. Or on nights like December 13.

Ah, that night . . .

Even if you stopped asking me for answers, the questions would still take up half of my nonexistence. Lightning flashed outside. My wife had gone over to the window again and I meant to ask her: what are you trying to locate? On the other side of the windowpane there was nothing but darkness and desolation. But I never managed to question her because I was already falling asleep. It was a kind of unhealthy torpor streaked with snowflakes through which I could barely make out the shape of my first lover, the partisan girl, and, at her side, my bodyguard. He was there as he had been forty years before when, in the highlands, as we were trying to escape from our nationalist enemies, I lay in mortal fever, and begged them both, my lover and my bodyguard, to finish me off. Kill me, I begged them, but don't let me fall into their hands . . . They looked at me as if they had been turned to stone. My fever had turned them into spectral figures, who now split into three, and now merged into a single fearsome creature, half man and half woman.

It was when my wife moved away from the window and drew closer to me that I saw her in the shape of my first lover, the one I was never able to marry. And she came this time as she had done forty years earlier with my old bodyguard . . . Silently, they both stepped nearer, then the guard stood back and only she was there, in the mist, but again in duplicate, simultaneously lover and wife — a bicorporal woman who instead of bringing me a cup of chamomile tea was pointing the black mouth of a gun barrel straight at me. I didn't feel the slightest fear, I even thought: why did I have to wait four decades for them to hear my prayer? Kill me, I thought then as I had done before, don't let me fall into their hands! And then all of a sudden everything went blank.

I have now been floating in the void for years, carried here and there by inconstant winds. I suspect I am moving, and yet I stay still; I seem to be standing still and yet I am dashing I know not where. And to cap it all, in this bottomless and boundless space, in this desperate vastness where one soul meets another only too rarely — in the midst of this void, as I've told you again and again, we successors, escorted by our retinues, are, like the guides among us, no more than a paltry handful of pitiful beings.

You try in vain to unscramble our signs. To understand the motives of one or another among us. But we, who are both guides and successors, now and forever more reunited, embrace and throttle each other, we tire ourselves out trying to tear off each other's heads, with equal anger. If I had been the Guide, I would have inflicted the same fate on him; he and I would have ended up changing places dozens of times, as many times as similar events came to recur throughout all eternity. That's why I felt no rest or reassurance when I saw his statue torn down by the crowd and his bronze head shattered. Only sterile grieving, resembling everything else that surrounds me in these funereal regions where I am condemned to wander without end.

That is how we are.

That is why you have no cause to lament or feel any regret. And even less cause to expect us to reappear in the form of medieval ghosts hovering over museums and fortresses, demanding that our sons take revenge. We were impossible fathers, and so we could only have impossible wives, sons and daughters.

Don't try to work out where we went wrong. We are but the offspring of a great disorder in the universe. And as we came into the world, by mistake, in accursed cohorts, on each other's coattails, with one of us now in the lead, now in second place, now Guide and now Successor, so we began our long march through blood and ashes toward you.

We never knew prayers or repentance, so don't ever think of lighting candles for the salvation of our souls. You'd be better off praying for something else. Pray that as we gyrate to no end in the dark abyss of the universe, we never happen to spy in the blackness and far distance the light of the terrestrial globe, and — like cutthroats who happen on the village where they were born— we exclaim: oh, but that's

Earth! Otherwise, like those assassins who turn off their path to visit their first home, we might also make a detour and, pitiless and unrepentant, masked and bloodstained as we always were and always will be, we might return to bring you new misfortunes, sans amen.

Tirana–Paris
October 2002–March 2003

THE PENELOPIAD

MARGARET ATWOOD

In Homer's *Odyssey*, Penelope is portrayed as the quintessential faithful wife, her story a salutary lesson through the ages. In a splendid contemporary twist to the ancient tale, Margaret Atwood has chosen to give the telling of it to Penelope, asking: 'What was she really up to?'

"*Penelope flies with the help of the sardonic, dead-pan voice Atwood lends her, a tone half Dorothy Parker, half* Desperate Housewives."
Boyd Tonkin, *Independent*

"[An] *exquisitely poised book.*" Lucy Hughes-Hallett, *Sunday Times*

£7.99

1 84195 704 6 (10-digit ISBN); 978 1 84195 704 3 (13-digit ISBN)

WEIGHT

JEANETTE WINTERSON

Condemned to shoulder the world, for ever, by the gods he dared defy, freedom seems unattainable to Atlas. But then he receives an unexpected visit from Heracles, and it seems they can strike a bargain that might release him. *Weight* turns the familiar on its head to show us ourselves in a new light.

"A *touching meditation on the difficult journey to self-knowledge, and also extremely funny.*" Lucasta Miller, *Guardian*

£6.99

1 84195 775 5 (10-digit ISBN); 978 1 84195 775 3 (13-digit ISBN)

www.canongate.net

THE PEOPLE'S ACT OF LOVE

JAMES MEEK

1919, Siberia. Under the military rule of a demented Kurtz-like commander, a shunned Christian community practises its esoteric religion. Then Samarin arrives, apparently having escaped from Russia's northernmost prison camp and being pursued by a cannibal known only as 'The Mohican'. When the local shaman is found dead, suspicion and terror engulf the little town.

"The People's Act of Love *has a timeless quality; it will be read, referenced, studied and talked about for years to come.*" Irvine Welsh

"A *quite extraordinary novel.*" Philip Pullman

£7.99

1 84195 706 2 (10-digit ISBN); 978 1 84195 706 3 (13-digit ISBN)

THE PURE LAND

ALAN SPENCE

Aberdeen 1858: a restless nineteen-year-old boy is itching to escape the restrictive atmosphere of his native city. His ticket comes in the form of the offer of a job in Japan. So begins the rise of Thomas Blake Glover, from lowly shipping clerk to the millionaire industrialist whose expertise establishes Nagasaki as a crucial shipbuilding base, ironically making it a perfect target for the atomic bomb.

"*Spence is a visionary.*" Ali Smith

"*He is a writer to cherish, one offering deep and fulfilling pleasures.*" Allan Massie

£12.99

1 84195 855 7 (10-digit ISBN); 978 1 84195 855 3 (13-digit ISBN)

www.canongate.net